Rooney's Shorts

Rooney's Shorts

William Rooney

Harrington Park Press
An Imprint of The Haworth Press, Inc.
New York • London • Oxford

Published by

Southern Tier Editions, Harrington Park Press, an imprint of The Haworth Press, Inc., 10 Alice Street, Binghamton, NY 13904-1580

Cover design by Jennifer M. Gaska.

Cover photo © 1999 Bent Light.

Library of Congress Cataloging-in-Publication Data

Rooney, William.
   Rooney's shorts / William Rooney.
      p. cm.
   ISBN 1-56023-954-9 (alk.)—1-56023-150-5 (pbk.)
   1. Gay men—Social life and customs—Fiction. 1. Title.
   PS3568.0634R6 1999
   813'.54—dc21
                                                99-10329
                                                CIP

CONTENTS

Boy of Bright Green Age   1

The Magic of a Provincetown Night   7

Patrick from Jamaica   17

Outlaws   23

Cocksucker with a Gun   33

A Refugee from the Ocean   47

Ocean Boy   63

The Shih Tzu Master's Thermos   81

The Moon Again   93

Marilyn: The Last Performance   101

Manifest Destiny Magazine   111

Survival on the Glacial Slide   133

Boy of Bright Green Age

All his stepfather had to do was open his eyes as he lay stretched out on the couch and he would see the boy.

That was the thrill.

To stand in the late-night hour of the room lit dimly by an outside corner streetlamp. Naked. And so close to the snoring man's body.

Used to be his stepfather went upstairs to bed with his mother every night at the same early time, but not anymore. Tonight was the same as a lot of nights. The boy knew the man had been drinking too much wine and that he would be here passed out on the sofa. Fully dressed except for his feet, which stuck out over the arm of the couch. So close, the naked boy could reach out and touch the man's toes.

He thought back to about a year ago and how he had almost asked his stepfather about something. But he had decided that he had better not ask. He did not like the man, and the question had to do with deformity. He had had to secretly consult books in the library because if he could not ask his stepfather, who could he ask? After much studying up on the subject, he had been relieved that he had solved the mystery himself. He had felt like a little jerk when he found the answer. He must have been the slowest boy on the block. He had actually thought the thing sticking out from between his legs was a giant tapeworm. This was the hard-on the other kids his age joked about. He used to laugh along with the other kids when they joked about hard-ons, but the truth was, he had had no idea what they were talking about.

He had been awfully young a year ago.

Standing there now, watching his stepfather's face and knowing he could open his eyes at any second. See the thing he would not tell him about pointing like a gun straight at his head.

But although he did not want to—at a time like this—he found himself thinking of the past again. About when he was seven— the year his father had died. About how his mother had married this man one year later. The boy was an only child, and his mother had let this man come to live with them.

He had come to live with them just one year after his father's death, and he was noisy and into things all over the house. He seemed to be everywhere. Making the house his own. Sitting at the head of the table. Talking, talking, talking. Laughing way too loud when there was nothing funny to laugh at. Eating with slurpy noises and dominating the TV.

The boy never really cared about the TV—he was a reader— but it was the fact that the stepfather made the TV his own that bothered him. Like he made everything his own. Like his mother. And the rest of the house that still belonged to his father.

In the beginning, he tried to play with the boy. Tried to play ball with him in the yard. Box with him in the house. And these efforts filled the boy with disgust.

Then when he was nine, his mother had a baby boy, and the stepfather no longer tried to play with him so much. He was on his way now to filling the house with his own people.

Staring at the man's face, he watched the eyelids flutter. He could open his eyes, and then what? He could open his eyes and see him standing here like this.

Wouldn't that be something?

Lately he has been slipping out the bedroom window and onto the third-floor roof late at night. He lies out there naked on a blanket. Knowing that it is different now. The change in his body— if they saw him—would greatly upset people.

There was a thrill in the chance that someone would see him. That's all he knew. Somehow it was fun that they could see him like this.

He is thirteen now and actually has very little to do with his stepfather. He has built his own new world. His father had taught him to read before he was five, and he has loved reading so much that recently he has begun to write his own stories. Since he began reading adult novels, they have filled him in on everything he needs to know about sex. And so he writes sex books.

He knew that sex was all everyone ever thought about. Including himself anymore. The other kids he knew bragged about conquests with girls, and mostly he did not believe that they ever did what they said they did. He never bragged. Never talked about sex to anyone. What he did was write a novel about a boy who couldn't stop masturbating.

The Catholic Church said that masturbation was a sin. The Catholic Church seemed to think that all of sex itself was a sin. And he used to confess his own limited contribution to the evil world of sex to a priest every week.

But he did not go to confession anymore. What was the point? You confessed. Said penance. Swore not to do it again. And then went back the following week to confess the very same sin. Were you supposed to do this every week for the rest of your life? Why not confess to breathing also?

At the age of thirteen, he was completely bored by the Catholic Church.

Maybe it was all a sin but everyone did it.

And something else.

He had something now that he had not had as a little kid. Something like power.

It was as though he had entered a world of chance. A nervous world where he was a part of all anyone ever thought about.

He knew people now. And they were all the same.

A few months ago, he had ridden on a subway train that had been so crowded he could not move. He had stood crushed within the crowd of people and a hand had cupped itself over his crotch. This had happened while he was feeling tense because the train had been going much too fast. It was an express, but it had been blasting through stations at unnatural speed—rocking the passengers against one another. He had really believed they could all be killed, and then came the hand.

The hand that knew him so well. And he forgot about the danger of the careening train. He blew up in the hand that knew he had been waiting for this moment.

The train finally slowed to come into his station and the hand was still there.

For the first time, he looked up to see who had done this to him.

A man about the same age that his father had been when he died.

He looked into the man's eyes, and the eyes were full of fear.

He was no longer just a kid.

He scared people now.

He got off the train and the man did not follow. And he was relieved when he did not follow. But now he had the problem of what he showed. People could see. Should he let them see? Let certain ones see?

No. He took off his sweater and wrapped it around his waist so he was hidden.

You saved these things.

His father knew him as a little boy when he was passive and dependent. They took walks together, hand in hand.

His father had been sick so much of the time that the boy had had to remind himself constantly to walk slowly. If he walked too quickly he could cause his father to have another heart attack.

They would walk down a sidewalk shadowed by elms on a sunny day. And through spaces between the leaves, the sun splashed down upon the sidewalk. Walking together under the green and dark of the trees, he would play a game of trying to get his father to time his slow steps. Make his father's feet touch the sun spots on their walk down the street together.

But then there came a time when his father could no longer play the sun spot game—and went away to what the boring Catholic Church called heaven.

There were lots of family prayers to make sure his father made it up there all right. But no way of knowing if he ever arrived.

Then during that same year—even while those special-delivery-type family prayers were still being said—this man began to show up at the house to visit his mother.

To fill the house with noise and make the house his own.

So for years and years, the boy had lived in exile. There was nothing he could do.

Tonight, instead of slipping out to the roof naked, he had surprised himself by coming downstairs.

Knowing his stepfather would be passed out on the couch. Having noticed how much wine he had drunk tonight.

He knew that, anymore, he filled the house just as much as his stepfather, who would rather drink wine than go upstairs early with his mother.

He knew what his stepfather was made of.

The same thing all men are made of.

He stood there looking at him stretched out on the couch.

If he opened his eyes now.

The snoring stopped as though he sensed a presence.

If he opened his eyes now.

The boy took a step closer and rested his heavy penis on the man's foot.

His stepfather stirred—shifted on the couch.

The boy walked to the other end of the couch and rested his penis—even harder now than it had been before—right upon his stepfather's forehead.

Stood there looking down at him.

Watched his stepfather's eyes open a crack.

Looked down on his face.

His eyes through the cracks.

Stood there with his hard penis on the man's forehead.

Watched the eyes open wide.

And the boy smiled wide with a boyish grin.

The Magic of a Provincetown Night

A history of no more than a few hours between them, they roll down the hill together across September grass, yellow like the moon above, laughing in tumbles over rocks and wood and finally over an embankment wall—wham!—a drop of six feet onto the pavement of Standard Street out there on the crazy tip of Cape Cod, and thinking all this screamingly funny, they get up and limp and hobble across the street where they fall down the stairs of a basement bar, knowing they will not be refused drinks because this is Provincetown and diplomatic immunity prevails for all who seek asylum from the repression of sobriety.

He springs to his feet—light—the body of a young man not yet fully developed. He extends two skinny tanned arms, and the short athletic girl grips the unexpectedly large hands to rise laughing at the sound of his grunt.

Minutes later they face each other on bar stools—naked knees below their shorts, head to head as though exchanging confidences.

"God!" she gushes—a bit throaty, like her favorite actress—"I'm glad we met! You're just what I need tonight. A good drinking buddy and no complications."

With an exaggerated sigh meant to equal her theatrics, he says, "I'm doing pretty damn good for someone who doesn't drink. You know, I may have hit on something tonight. A strategy of heavy drinking as an antidote against poisonous relationships." He holds up the Cape Codder—vodka and cranberry juice.

She clinks his glass with her own Cape Codder. "That's an antidote old as time. To hell with love!" she says cheerfully, and they both down half their glasses. "Now if we could just get your boyfriend and my girlfriend to move in with each other, you and I could take a place and stay happily smashed the rest of our lives."

Laughing, he asks, "How old did you say you were? Twenty-two?"

"I tollllld you, Steve! Twenty-one! Same as you. Look at you. First real binge and already your memory's impaired."

"Okay, okay. Now! We were having this serious discussion back in that last bar." He pauses, then laughs. "It was very profound, whatever it was, and I can't remember a single word of what it was we said. Is your leg okay?"

She is reaching down near her ankle. "A little sore. I probably twisted my ankle, which means I'll need another drink right after this one to kill the pain."

He looks down at her head, dipped to inspect the ankle. Such healthy shiny hair. Short. Brunette. Her hands clutch his knees to steady herself on the bar stool, and it is like the familiar touch of an old friend. Although a few nerves do somersaults up through his thighs.

Suddenly the head bobs up. The large brown eyes that he has come to trust bore into the small blue eyes that she sees as safe—childish. "Oh! I know! We were talking about me. I was wondering back there if it might all be a mistake. Women. I was wondering if I met the right hetero man, would it change me. If I wanted to be changed."

A chance to hold forth. There is something in her manner that does not take him seriously. "Yeah, right. You said that. But no, Joann, I don't think so. I mean, you could get into a relationship with a guy, but that wouldn't necessarily end it with women. 'Cause it's all animal. 'Cause you've been there with women, see? A dog raids a chicken coop and knocks off a few chickens, you got a chicken-killing dog on your hands for life. No matter how domestic that dog may be, once he knows the taste of chicken blood . . . whatta you laughing at?"

"You're comparing my sex life to drinking chicken blood. Geeezus, Steve!" And they are both laughing for a minute, but then abruptly she changes—looks off into space—pouting. "Anyway you slice it though, it's all a mess. Sex. All a mess. Not the act, but the minds behind the act."

"Maybe, but it's all we have."

"Not really. What about you and me? Right here—right now? It's so nice. I think people who do without sex must get along just fine."

"I couldn't do that. Go without it."

"Oh sure you could."

"You ever think about children?"

"If I ever feel a biological vacancy inside me, then I'm gonna have children. But I would never let them defrost some guy's stuff and stick it inside me. There's something so TV-dinnerish about that. In a few years they'll be selling sperm in the frozen food section of the supermarkets."

"So you'd screw with a guy? What if your girlfriend didn't approve?"

"I'd just get her to realize that this is for us. That this is our baby I'm working on. I'd tell her how important it is to me that our baby come out of direct human contact and not from a refrigerator in a laboratory. I mean, Christ! A baby like that has hand job written all over it."

"Well, I'll tell you what, Joann. If we still know each other when your biological vacancy becomes apparent, you can use my body. As long as I can kinda slip in and out fast." He is immediately embarrassed. Did the joke sound like a come-on?

Smiling at his red face, she says, "Chivalry in the modern age. You would actually offer a lady your penis."

"I have no interest in children myself. I just wanna have a lot of dogs."

Easy to picture him at home with a yard full of dogs. He seems a little too shy for the real world. Weak bravado. And yet maybe not. In spite of his face, which seems to have been physically arrested at seventeen, there is the weight of a dominant man in the deep voice. And the way he picked her up after they fell down the hill—those quick, big hands. He's such a mix. Dark hair that looks and falls so much like her own—sensitive blue eyes and such smooth, unblemished skin. A really nice, polite boy—a perfect brother. But then there is the large hooked nose and again—those hands. Believable when he said he couldn't do without sex. The guys must love him.

"So how long have you been with David?"

"Two years next week."

"Little more than two for Carrie and me." Staring into space again. "I love her, but she can be a total douche bag. Ain't easy to live with at all."

"Neither is David. Unless it's me. To this day, it's hard for me to get used to habits unlike my own."

"A lot of people really should live alone."

"Oh, I don't think anyone wants to live alone. Not really."

"I think I could live alone."

"Not me." He smiles apologetically—not wanting to say it, but here it is anyway. "I think too much about dying when I'm alone."

"You're twenty-one, for God's sake! And you think about dying?"

"Well, it's all around us, almost as much as living is."

"You mean AIDS."

"Not just AIDS. Time. I mean, when I'm alone, I think how fast the first twenty-one years went. And then I think, if the rest of my life is like that, it's gonna be over in a blink."

"Yes, but if you're healthy, you'll probably live for a—"

"That doesn't change the fact that every moment we live we're also dying." He realizes he has taken her hand. "How did we get on this anyway? Maybe we should go roll down the hill again." And then takes his hand away.

A healthy young guy like this afraid of dying. How honest of him to say that. She is so afraid of cancer that she won't even allow it into their conversation. "How drunk are you?" she asks.

"I seem to go in and out of it."

"I think we could both be drunker. Let's have another drink." She signals the bartender who comes down from the other end of the bar to say that last call was ten minutes ago. "Damn!" she says.

"Let's go to my place. I have vodka and cranberry juice. I bought it this afternoon when I decided to get drunk, but I didn't last long drinking at home alone. Still got a lot left." He then regrets having made the suggestion. You can't invite a stranger over to your house at this hour of the night. Especially to drink. It was all so casual and easy up till now, but isn't she going to think he's up to sex even if he is queer? What an oddball situation.

"As long as there's no chance David will come home. He sounds like the type who'd jump to the wrong conclusion. I know Carrie would."

"He's in New York, but if it makes you nervous to come over, I under—"

"No, I'm not nervous if it's just you and me and not a jealous lover with a chain saw. We can stay up all night talking like I used to in college with my girlfriends." And there he goes again with his red face.

In the living room of the cottage, she sits on the beat-up sofa, grilling herself while he makes drinks in the unpartitioned kitchen area. She wants to lift her leg up on the sofa because her ankle hurts, but she doesn't want him to be concerned. How stupid. Why is she being so uncomfortably brave? She keeps her two feet planted on the floor so he won't notice the swelling. She would not even allow herself to limp during the walk over, even though it hurt so much to put weight on the leg. Why doesn't she just ask for a damn ice pack?

He brings the drinks into the living room. Made them strong in an effort to recapture some of the ease they had back in the bar. Walking over here to the cottage, they were too quiet. But to make potent drinks in a situation like this. . . . Ahhh! He's sick of thinking about it. He has to loosen up. And he reminds himself that he is a hornball gay man who's been driven to distraction over all the beautiful men in the world for almost a decade now.

There is only one dim lamp on, and as he sits across from her in a creaking rocking chair, he considers music, but then rain begins to fall. The windows are open and the warm September rain comes down lightly. She sighs peacefully, "Oh, that sounds so nice, doesn't it?"

"Yeah," he says softly, and they both sip long from their glasses. Rain like this—on a ground of fall's first leaves always reminds him of childhood. Something about the smell of damp leaves can make him remember the way he felt at five and six when he was like a puppy. Curious about everything. His nose in a handful of autumn leaves. Melancholy in the beauty of decay. And now he has a sense of transience. This night with his new friend will be over too soon. As though they had simply ducked into the cottage for shelter from the rain for a few lonely moments.

She looks over at him, wondering why he is sad. "I'm just thinking about how David and Carrie would get along. Maybe we'll all have dinner some night. I mean, if we all patch things up."

"Yeah, that'd be nice."

"You have any solid evidence on him? I mean, all you said was that he seemed to have a wandering eye lately."

"Well, we were each other's first. Late bloomers or something. Anyway, we never used condoms, and then one day I found he was carrying them in his wallet. Couldn't have been for him and me."

She stares into his eyes, feeling so bad for him. David is on his way out. He looks so depressed, as though he is just now realizing there can be no doubt about what David is up to these days. "You're too far away. Come over here," she commands, surprising herself with this sudden maternal instinct.

He gets up from the rocking chair and sits down next to her— smiles affectionately at her compassion. And then looks sheepish as her arm goes around his shoulders. He shouldn't have cut so close to his own bone with such an intimate indictment of David. He could have shown a little reserve in a personal matter. He could have made the drinks a lot weaker is what it probably is.

"How 'bout you and Carrie?" he asks, hoping to bury the embarrassment of his own position.

"Well, I told you I saw her turning on the charm for this new waitress. I don't really know if she ever went with her or not. What really hurts is that Carrie's ten years older than I am and I've always felt like a baby with her, and now suddenly she's coming on to an eighteen-year-old kid. Suddenly I feel so fucking old!" She laughs. "I mean, I know how superficial that sounds, but I feel like a wrinkled-up old prune at twenty-one!" And she is appalled when she begins to laugh again and feels tears running down her face.

She removes her arm from his shoulders and uses both hands to dry her eyes. "Hell with both of 'em," he says, and throws his arm around her. The way it should be. Feeling chipper, he strokes the back of her head protectively.

But she recovers quickly and turns her face to him with a grin. "You feel so mature and on top of things when a relationship is going well. And then when it begins to fall apart, you feel like this pimply ugly kid no one wants to play with anymore."

"Well, you can always play with me"—and kisses her on the lips, thinking that it was just an irresistible thing to say and he had to kiss her, with her face so close, and wanted to kiss her too. And then slides her down on the couch while her legs rise to lay and then, losing his nerve, buries his mouth in the hollow above her collarbone.

"Uh oh," she says. "We got trouble."

On top of her—murmuring—"It was inevitable," and somehow thinking of those wet leaves outside and how this was the answer to that sad way they made him feel.

"I guess so. I guess it was inevitable. Do you really want to? I mean, I want to, but you must admit it's a little freaky."

He smiles. "Like we're some kind of traitors to our people? Like we're defaming the lambda?"

Her face moves a bit and she kisses his neck. He can feel her lips part in a smile, and then she says, "What if it opens doors? A whole new outlook."

"What if once we try it we can't stop? They have rehabs for this kind of thing?"

"Is there such a thing as funny sex?"

And he is laughing now into her neck. "I don't know. When I think of all the years of training that went into being a decent queer . . . when I think of all I wanted to be . . ."

Laughing. "I've hardly even begun with women. I really believed I was on to something."

"You won't blame me will you? For twisting you out of shape?
You won't start drinking a lot and talking about all you could've
been?"

"Let's be serious for a minute. What if the body says yes and
the mind says no?"

"Crucial philosophical decision."

"Yes. You make it."

He tilts to the side and props up on one elbow—head in hand.
"I think maybe we already decided."

She stares past him at the ceiling. "Think a couple of years from
now we'll look back and regret it? Not going through with it?"

"Probably. This seemed so free. Not many things seem that
way to me. But you know something? I felt lousy before and now
I don't. I feel really good now. Almost as though we went
through with it."

"I know what you mean. This feels like the comfortable way
you feel after sex."

He smiles. "I really like you, Joann."

"I think I found myself a buddy tonight."

He shifts to lie beside her, and hearing the low sigh of pain he
asks, "What's wrong?"

"My damn ankle."

Looking down the length of her—"Oh, man! Why didn't you
say something? It's all blue and swollen."

"I didn't wanna ruin things. In spite of both of us getting depressed and everything, I was actually having a good time."

"Do you think it's broken?"

"No. I walked over here, didn't I? It's just a bad sprain. If you
can get me an ice pack. . . . What's the matter, Steve?"

He carefully moves across her and onto his feet. Looking
down at her ankle, he says, "I guess we were really drunk."

"So? What's so tragic about that?"

"I dunno. I don't wanna think of tonight as one of those
sloppy-drunk nights people talk about. You know. When they

wake up in the morning and disown everything they did just because they were drunk. I hate that."

She is up leaning on her elbows. "Oh, Steve, c'mon . . ."

"I mean, while we were connecting, your ankle was disconnecting. Like there was this fault running through our time together."

"Steeeeeeeve . . ." God, he's young. So unsure. Lost. But in a strange, nice way. "The ice pack can wait. Sit down here a minute. Come on." Patting the space she has made next to herself.

He sits, shaking his head. "Ach! Sorry! Now you know why David's looking for a replacement."

"Fuck David."

And he is a little shocked as he looks into her eyes. And then laughs. Really laughs hard, and she is laughing too.

The phone rings and he blinks nervously. But she lies back with her arms folded behind her head, watching the glint of hope in his eyes.

When he answers, his end of the conversation sounds like the code a stranger in the room always hears when it's two intimate people on the phone. She gets up from the sofa and hobbles to the refrigerator to make an ice pack, and by the time she returns to the sofa, he has hung up the phone. She has her leg up on a chair with the ice pack around her ankle, and he returns to stand there looking down at her leg.

She looks up at him. "Glad he's coming home?"

And he laughs, embarrassed and excited. "Yeah."

"That's good. I'm just happy you're happy."

"I can get some blankets. Make you comfortable there for the night."

"Okay. We can talk some more." And then looking past him with that faraway gaze. "Ah, shit. Can you bring me the phone? I'll get Carrie to come over and get me."

Patrick from Jamaica

His index finger—white and trembling—traced the circumference of the scar on the black hairless forearm. The black man was short and his brown eyes looked up into the blue eyes of the white man, and he whispered in a voice reserved for sacred matters, "Now feel inside."

The white man's finger slid inside the scar where the bone had caved from the impact of the bullet. His finger explored, caressed the difference in the texture of flesh. Membranous inside the scar. He thought of the soft spot on an infant's head, and because it was humid in the tropical night and the man's arm was damp, he thought—or had the sense of—intimate touch inside warm, wet tissue. The nervous sensual thrill of touching the wound of the violated.

They stood alone on a fire escape landing outside the hotel, and the branches of an areca palm tree formed a canopy not too far above their heads. A breeze came off the nearby ocean and the thick leaves of the areca made a snapping sound, as though someone were shuffling cards above the fire escape. The breeze struck the outer leaves, and the successive sound of one leaf after another snapping startled the New Englander as though someone was watching. A dealer ready to disperse the deck.

*　*　*

The New Englander had had a hard time adjusting to co-workers from Latin America. He had always thought of himself as an unprejudiced liberal, yet the multicultural maze that was life in South Florida had disoriented and irritated him upon his arrival. And when he had landed a job as bartender in a luxury hotel, the fact that he did not understand Spanish had thrown him into the alienated mood of a man in exile. He even wondered if the Hispanics talked about him while they worked around him.

But it was the Jamaicans—of which there were many on the staff—who most affected the latent redneck in his personality. They spoke English, but it only tantalized because they rushed through words with a whoosh—a sound so fast it was incomprehensible. They were a domineering people with seemingly over-stimulated brains in need of windfalls of words to express themselves—pause to reload and then cut loose with another volley. Not that they fired their communications at the New Englander all that often. Most often he found himself ignored, except that one young man (with the body of a twelve-year-old boy) gave the impression of seeking him out for no apparent reason. This would have sounded the only friendly note to the New England-er's abused ears were it not for the fact that the Jamaican unfailingly left him in the Caribbean smoke of a staccato rhythm he did not understand. Also, the young man addressed him with the same aggressive punch of attitude as the other Jamaicans. He was left with the feeling that the guy was at least trying to be sociable, and yet the New Englander still remained apart in his frustration and irascibility.

He had been working at the hotel for a week when he came back one night after a day off and simply did not want to be there anymore. He had spent a part of his free time on the phone to Boston with friends, and he had less taste than before for the foreign environment of the hotel. The sound of Spanish chatter ate through to his psyche like a flurry of termites. The Jamaicans seemed to wish for nothing more than to goad him into a fight. There were too many immigrants in this fucking country.

Early in the evening, he had served drinks for a reception, and the tray that stood on a stand next to the bar was filled with empty glasses. This annoyed him because it was part of the waiter's duties to take the tray back to the dishwasher every time it filled with empties. As the reception ended, he stood there glaring at the dirty tray when the young Jamaican man walked by.

Passing by the bar, one arm lifted and balancing a tray of dirty dishes, the Jamaican gestured at the tray of glasses with his free hand, simultaneously pulling the trigger on a round of angry communication that sounded like "Take your glasses to the kitchen yourself! Waiters have no time!"

He nailed the waiter with a look hard enough to invoke worry in the brown eyes and quicken his step toward the kitchen. And then the New Englander came around the bar and followed the Jamaican into the kitchen and all the way to the dishwasher's station in back. The man put the tray of dishes down and whirled to say, "Whatsamattah with you, man?"

"Look! First of all, I want you to know that I haven't understood a word you've said to me since I got here! And second, don't ever try to give me another fucking order again!"

He expected a blast of incomprehensible retaliation—possibly even a fistfight. The Jamaicans seemed so angry all the time anyway, he thought for sure that his words would really blow the lid off things. But all he received back from the Jamaican standing in front of him was a completely dumbfounded expression. The man looked back at him with a question in his eyes. He could not, for the life of him, understand why the New Englander was so upset.

For the rest of that night and two that followed, he would not even look directly at the Jamaican. But his peripheral gaze noted quick inquisitive glances sent his way from the waiter. Histories, the New Englander thought. Histories so far apart he could not even guess what went on in the small dark country of his co-worker's head.

He took cigarette breaks out on the fire escape because no one ever went there. He could get away from the sounds of Spanish—of Jamaican patois. Tonight he stepped out into the seventy-five-degree air, weighing the argument for an immediate return to Boston. And a minute later, the young Jamaican stepped through the door.

There was not much room on the landing, and the two looked at each other. Willed blank faces. They were embarrassed. And then the Jamaican turned his back on the New Englander, lit a cigarette, and blew smoke into space.

Free to let his eyes roam, the New Englander noticed for the first time a subtle red tint to the dark hair. He stared intently to make sure the detail was not an illusion caused by the light—attached to the side of the building a few floors above—that filtered down through the leaves of the areca. He decided the hair actually did possess a reddish hue. And he remembered how one night he thought he heard amidst a blast of Jamaican speech a vague Irish lilt when the young man spoke. It was an unusual moment, for he had been amused—struck by a recurring thought he had had since moving to South Florida and hearing from time to time a mix of accents gathered in one individual's voice. Our mothers of the world have always gotten around a whole lot more than we like to believe.

The Jamaican had a thin neck—delicate. He bent forward with arms placed on the railing. He spoke out into the night, slowly said, "Tough job tonight. I'm tired." Slow, with pauses between the words.

They were both wearing the hotel's dress—black shoes and pants, white tuxedo shirts, black vests and ties. And maybe it was because the Jamaican leaned forward on the rail, causing his clothes to hug the small body, that the New Englander felt concil-iatory. And then there was the paced-out sentence he had uttered, which could be construed as a peace offering. So the New En-glander answered, "They're all tough nights in this place. Some-times it's a battlefield." Studying the boyish contour spooned out from the railing with the vulnerability of a diver taking the plunge.

Again the Jamaican spoke slowly, "Sometimes I stay away. Don't answer the phone. Don't come in."

So strange to hear, but it was there. The Irish inside the Jamai-can patois. The New Englander said, "I don't know your name."

"Patrick."

"I'm Sean. My middle name is Patrick."

Patrick turned from the railing a little too quickly. Actually he spun around—disturbing the stillness of the night. He laughed, "Maybe we are related. But I don't think so." A rush of words. "Chocolate. Vanilla. Do you know what annoys me? When they call the dessert white chocolate. There cannot be white chocolate dessert."

Coming from Boston—a city with a vicious racist history—he did not quite know how to construe the last remark. So he said, "Do you miss Jamaica? Ever go back?"

His speech slowed. "Jamaica is a very beautiful place. More flowers than anywhere in the Caribbean." He undid the button of his cuff on the right arm and rolled up his sleeve—held the arm up for Sean to see. There was an ugly, sunken scar halfway between wrist and elbow. He laughed, seemed tickled and wondrous as he said, "I went home a year ago and some crazy man in a bar shot me. I still cannot believe he shot me."

Sean thought that he would have to live inside disorientation for as long as he remained in contact with these people. The excited face was looking up at him expectantly—the eyes shone so brightly. Patrick appeared to be both puzzled and oddly delighted that he had been shot.

"There was a reason? I mean, was there an argument?"

"No! There was no argument!" He took a step closer, eyes wide with disbelief and great amusement. "I was sitting in a bar in Kingston. He came in and started shooting! I never saw him before in my life." But then his head dipped—he stared down at his shoes and in a somber, low tone of voice said, "You never know, man. You never know." He paused for nearly a minute and still looking down asked, "You are married? Do you have children?"

The abrupt change of subject—the question itself—left him feeling exposed somehow as he answered, "No, I'm not married."

Patrick came closer—the arm raised for inspection—eyes now burned into Sean's eyes. "Look at the work they did on this arm! Put your finger on it and you feel how it is like a sinkhole!" Demanding, but with something like camaraderie in the tone, as though telling Sean to bear witness. To the insanity of having been shot. To the absurdity of bad stitch work. He took the last step he could take—their clothes brushed and now Patrick's eyes held some haunted question. He took Sean's hand and placed it on his arm. "Feel how my bone is caved in."

His hand playing lightly over Patrick's arm but not yet touching the scar, he at first wanted to ask the color of the gunman. But then as his finger began to trace around the scar—trembling with the intimacy of the moment—he felt that the question of the gunman was not worth asking. He brought his other hand up to hold the young man by the wrist while his finger moved around the scar.

"Now feel inside."

His finger slid into thin, new skin damp from sweat, and he touched and soothed while with his other hand he could feel Patrick's pulse quicken.

The quick snapping sound of the areca leaves caused by a sudden breeze off the ocean made them both tense for a moment. Someone shuffling cards just above their heads. His finger inside the place where the bullet had entered. He let the tip of his finger rest. Indecisive. He looked into the now familiar eyes of the Jamaican, warm and amused. And he smiled into the brown eyes while the wind blew and the shuffling sound of the leaves spoke of a game still to be played.

Outlaws

On his own now, he spent more time outside exploring the beach and woods with the dog. He tried his hand at painting—sought to capture the brilliance of light that had always drawn artists to the Cape. But he found himself, at forty, too impatient to develop a beginner's skills. It would take a long time to become a decent painter, and ever since his diagnosis, he never allowed himself long-term plans.

He took the dog for long walks—always hoping to spot animals. He was tickled by the speed of rabbits and Steve's half-hearted attempt to pursue. Amazed by the single-file walk of a fox—steps designed to leave a singular trail of prints to throw off trackers. Fascinated by the curiosity of a seal one winter day while it swam in Nantucket Sound parallel to where Ed and Steve walked along the beach. The seal would bark—head bobbing above the choppy waves—and the dog would answer with his own bark. Ed had had the spooked and amused sense of watching two long-separated ancestors catching up on family gossip.

But it was the coyotes who were his special interest. They existed so cloaked in stealth that many people living on Cape Cod did not even know they were there. There were thousands of them, and after the high population of summer tourists departed, they reclaimed the freedom that had been abandoned in the spring. And they were experts at timing and camouflage—wild and yet living amid human society. They were outlaws sharing the land with unsuspecting landlords. When the wealthy humans retreated back to the city in the fall, their expensive lots were taken over by wild animals, and the people who remained for winter hardly knew that the properties were not vacant after all.

The coyotes were the largest of the wild animals, and they were a species whose aim it was to live unrecognized by the human race.

*   *   *

Ed and Frankie had moved from Boston to Hyannis in September—had managed to snap up a beautiful cottage on the beach at off-season rates. Frankie—his lover of two years—had lasted until December before deciding that the socially sparse life of a Cape winter resident was not to his liking. And he left because of what he said was Ed's "changed personality." He broke up the relationship—in actual fact—because he was twenty years younger than Ed and had felt no need whatsoever to try to slow time down by means of a stripped-down life. Ed did not blame Frankie for the way he thought. The move to the Cape had been Ed's idea, and although he had thought it more than possible that Frankie would fall for the beauty of the place, they had come here because Ed had wanted to live here all of his life.

As for the charge of a "changed personality," it had been undeniable. The first few months in the fall had been a bad time. Ed, a bartender in Boston gay bars all of his working life, could not find a job in a Cape gay bar. There was only one gay bar in the area, and he knew he had been turned down because he looked so much older than the clientele and the other bartenders. There was a plethora of bars in Provincetown—out on the eastern tip of the Cape—but a move out there was financially impossible. Provincetown had, over the years, become an expensive little place in which to live.

Rejection by the Hyannis bar hurt. He had been given notification that his desirability was on the wane. And it was not just his physical ego that had taken a hit—he began to panic at the thought of what he would do for work.

A few weeks after moving to the Cape, he bluffed his way into the only bar job available in Hyannis—a straight sports bar. He tried to look at his predicament as a new experience. He was nothing less than an actor now. For eight hours a day, he was somebody else. There was never any doubt in his mind that if the men who drank at the bar had any suspicion of his real identity, they would withdraw their patronage. Hyannis—off-season—was a small, old-fashioned town. An HIV-positive gay bartender was anathema to these people who looked upon Provincetown as a cesspool of disease.

A bartender lived on tips, and to suit the needs of the men who came to the sports bar, he bent the self he had always known. He joined in the locker-room jargon—the "pussy" jokes and so on. He smiled deliciously and whistled at any big-busted actress who crossed the TV screen above the bar. He was careful about the way he dressed when he went to work, and he let his hair grow over his ears just like his patrons. He reminded his eyes to behave themselves whenever he was drawn to a man drinking at the bar. All personal questions were answered with a fabricated history. Just about all of the conversations with the men at the bar had nothing to do with his real life.

He would come home from work—to Frankie—drained. Within weeks, he had found it hard to make the transition from the man he was at work to the man he had always been out of work. He actually had nights when he found it hard to show affection to Frankie—it seemed like such an effeminate thing to do. He lived for the time he spent on the beach and in the woods, camera slung around his neck and Steve the dog running ahead. Sex with Frankie was awkward. Ed, suddenly, was a horny man who took what he wanted and then jumped from bed to refrigerator for a can of beer and a look at TV for the latest sports news so he would know what to talk about at work the next day.

He knew Frankie was disgusted by the phony life he led. And he knew Frankie felt alone living with him. It was easy to understand Frankie's point of view when he told Ed that they had to go back to Boston. Frankie was bored with the Cape, and Ed's estrangement made the life out here intolerable to the younger man. But Ed would not leave. Because of time. He loved the Cape, and he feared that if he left, he might never return again. He no longer had the luxury of chalking up a segment of time as a false start.

Did he love a strip of sand more than a human being? Maybe not, but when your preoccupation was time, the predominant fear was of things and people slipping away. He could always count on waking to the smell of sea and sand if he stayed where he was. But could he always assume Frankie would be there beside him for all the years of decline that stretched ahead?

He had chosen the cottage for its view of wildlife from inside when the weather would turn cold. The place was a two bedroom nestled in a ravine about fifty yards from Nantucket Sound. After Frankie had returned to Boston and Ed found—to his relief—that he actually made enough at the bar to pay for the cottage on his own, he spent most of his time in the living room. One wall of the small room was composed of glass sliding doors that led out to a deck. He could sit in an armchair by the doors and enjoy a view of sand dunes that stretched upward to the south. He could look straight ahead to the west and a bit toward the north at a pond that nearly reached to below the outside deck. The dunes that led to the beach were covered with dense shrubs—a natural habitat for animals. And he had few neighbors in the area—most of the houses were vacant.

His temporary home (lasting until May when the summer rates would resume) made up for the meanness of the way he made a living. He had found a home off to the side of mainstream existence.

He missed Frankie, especially at night when he came home from work and the house was so still. He went through a period when he felt sorry for them both and thought about calling Frankie, asking if he felt like coming out to the cottage on weekends. But then solitude took possession of him—a kinship with his environment—the essence of which could not be shared with another human being. He had not been able to look at anything with a sense of newness for a long time, and now—amid the barren winter landscape of the Cape—he began to see movements among the animals that filled him with a vibrancy he had not known since childhood.

He walked with Steve at dawn one day along a snow-covered road, and they turned a bend to find a coyote staring at them from two hundred feet away.

The three animals froze in the road—all of them electric with surprise. The wind was blowing in Steve's direction, and he stood very still except for the nostrils of his nose, which quivered with all the possibilities of this confrontation. Looking down the road at the coyote, Ed thought he detected a profile in fear. But looking at Steve, the mood of the dog he had known for twelve years was one of wonder. Acute curiosity.

Fifteen thousand years of domesticity separated Steve from the coyote. If it had been another dog up the road, he would have been right up there checking him out as soon as he had spotted the animal. But something on the wind kept Steve rooted to his place next to Ed.

The two animals stared at each other, neither one moving— Steve well fed at fifty pounds, the coyote scrawny at thirty to thirty-five pounds. Steve was sand colored with clean white markings—maybe embarrassingly clean, as he confronted a wild and possibly more heroic relative. The coyote had an overgrown, dirty gray coat. And he would live for no more than seven years, while Steve could last for seventeen.

When the coyote finally trotted off, only a minute or two had passed, but Ed had caught the sense of standing on a road above the world—watching creatures watching each other across the millenniums that separated them.

He would sit by the sliding glass doors for hours with Steve at his feet and never think of himself. He would be so immersed in the drama of a wild blue heron standing with the aura of the prehistoric in the shallows of the pond. The bird could stand motionless for long periods of time, long beak like a sword, waiting to spear a fish. And because—in this tense stillness of the hunt—thinking seemed an intrusion, an actual noise, a sacrilegious tampering with the scales of life and death, any review of his own insignificant life was out of the question.

Two white swans would come into view and his head would fill with classical music. Families of ducks would appear looking like mongrel peasants living in the court of the elegant and majestic swans.

All would be quiet on a late winter afternoon. Something about the piercing winter light would throw Ed into a sterility of mood. Shadows—hints of mortality—would fall across the pond. He was growing old alone, and this last phase of the prime of his life was being wasted while he spent a third of his days with his true self buried deep enough so that no one would know.

And then off in the distance—on their way to the pond—he would hear the heraldic honk of geese, and he would smile because he had come to think of them as the bag ladies of the sky. When they landed, he could be on the other side of the cottage and still hear the loud thumping swoosh as they crashed the pond. They were large and noisy and very temperamental. They moved about on the pond looking deeply annoyed, and even on the most serene afternoon, they would honk their complaints and scowl at Ed when he walked out on the deck to watch them.

In April, newspapers and local TV broadcasts began to report that a rabies epidemic could appear on Cape Code. An epidemic already existed on mainland Massachusetts, and, therefore, vaccine bait had been laid along the canal that separated the Cape from the rest of the state. The idea was that animals crossing over to the Cape would eat the bait and become vaccinated before arriving on the other side. But now the worry was that bats were flying over to the Cape and bypassing the vaccine. Of special concern were the coyotes. The tourist season was beginning soon—families were on their way out to the Cape, and the businesspeople feared that any reports of rabid coyotes on the Cape might potentially destroy the summer's business.

Animal Control wanted to test wild animals for rabies. It was of special importance for residents to report any sightings of coyotes so that they could be brought in for testing.

A part of Ed's deck jutted out a few feet into the dunes that sloped upward from the cottage. A rowboat lay overturned and resting on bricks below the deck. It belonged to the owner and was of no interest to Ed until, one April morning, he realized a coyote family lived beneath the boat.

He had been on top of the dunes looking down at the cottage when he saw the male—a rabbit in his mouth—trotting along the shore of the pond. He was coming from the west, and as he drew near the overturned boat below the deck, four pups pounced out to meet him.

He wondered how long they had been living under the deck. Right there under his nose. Ed, the great observer of wildlife, had missed the most exciting show of all while it had taken place right outside the sliding doors. All those times he had walked out onto the deck he had never noticed anything. The coyotes had had, in effect, two ceilings, the boat and the deck. And he supposed that any sound from above—footsteps—was all the coyotes had needed to beat it back under the boat. But it was still amazing to him that he had never seen the male on his way to or from the hunt.

But now they became easier to observe—even from inside his living room. The pups were growing fast—they were restless and they strayed from beneath the boat to play in the dunes (though never more than ten yards from the boat). He had just a few weeks to watch them before he would have to leave the cottage because of escalating summer rent. He would have to find a cheap apartment in town where his wildlife observation days would come to an end until the fall. Like the coyotes, he would have to retreat from the shore with the influx of tourists.

He had thought that once the coyotes knew that they had been discovered, they would all move to some other hideout. The fact that they continued to live under the deck caused Ed to wonder if Steve and he had been observed by the animals through the winter. Didn't it show trust when the family did not move away? Some kind of pragmatic calculation that the two inside the cottage did not pose any danger? Then—watching the coyotes every day—Ed took his theory further. The animals sensed empathy in

Ed and compliance with his master's wishes in Steve. They were so vulnerable in the presence of the man and dog, as in full view the male coyote brought back food and the pups scrambled in play on the dunes. The life of this family was in the palm of his hand, and Ed believed that over the winter months a mystical alliance had formed on this plot of land where the cottage stood. The coyotes had come to know him without his ever having been aware that he shared a space with them. And now that they were exposed to his view, he found himself responsible for them.

But they had banked on his feeling that way. They had picked up on a camaraderie in his quiet movements. This was a man who, in his own way, assumed the role of a hunter out in the world but his movements when back at the den betrayed an animal practiced in the art of stealth. Coming home every night meant the hunt was over for the day. His quiet demeanor and the fact that his only companion was a dog were evidence of his exile from the deadly human race. He was not so far removed from their own strategies for survival. The way he lived his solitary life added up to a man who could only pass among other humans by means of disguise.

Ed wove this theory inside his psyche, and the line between the cottage and the boat was solidified. Just as the coyotes sensed it would happen, Ed thought of all the inhabitants of the ravine as copartners in survival.

The reminders would come across the nightly local news. Report any sighting of a coyote. So that they could be tested. So that precautions could be taken—a vaccination program implemented. Even though it had also made the news that the state did not have the money or the manpower to handle a real epidemic. To quote a man drinking at his bar one night—a man who loved to hunt—"Now, who's kiddin' who here? You get a rabies scare goin' and you spot a coyote who may or may not be sick, you sure as hell are not gonna call Animal Control. You know it'll take them all day to come. Fuck, man, you're better off playing it safe and blow that sucker's head off."

At the bar that night and on the local news there was never any discussion of raising the money so that more personnel could be hired at Animal Control. Manpower so that animals could be tested before destroying them. Money for vaccines to cover the area.

And Ed—who could be called quite a few names for the way he reasoned—watched the coyotes outside and thought about how people were not very good when confronted by disease. What they really wanted to do was simply get rid of the ones who had it.

One early morning in May—with just a week to go before he had to vacate the cottage—he watched the coyotes leave the boat. In another week, the summer tourists would start to arrive, and the female coyote led her pups west along the shore of the pond before they would turn north and into the camouflage of the woods for the next four to five months. He watched the pups as they rolled and tumbled and nipped at one another, and he knew that the male would follow later and find their new home.

And he was ready to leave also—had rented a small studio apartment right in the heart of downtown Hyannis where the rents were the least expensive. He accepted this condition with self-deprecating humor—or at least he tried to feel that way. No wild animals for three months, he wryly thought. It would be just Steve and himself among the civilized species.

But he did not realize, at first, that an instinctual shift was forming inside that place where change is not yet ready to reveal itself.

One night—soon after he had left the beach—he was talking to an attractive man at the bar about the Red Sox, and the self-restraint he had developed over the last nine months dissolved into a mischievous pool of absurdity. He suddenly found himself talking about pitching with a smile on his face while he mentally undressed the guy. And when his mate got up to play pool, Ed's gaze followed with appreciative scrutiny.

After that night, there were others who would catch his eye. His interest would perk when someone sexy came into the bar and he would feel eroticized. His juices would flow, and it became so that he looked forward to going to work, whereas he used to dread it.

He had no doubt that he would remain undetected. Until that day when he might choose to indicate what kind of animal he actually was (after storing enough nuts in the bank first), there was no way anyone could catch a man so well schooled in the art of invisible living while inside the circle of predators.

And, of course, he was a predator again now too. His nature had come out of hibernation and resumed its life behind the decoy of socially accepted behavior.

Cocksucker with a Gun

The gun was, of course, for self-defense. And when you lived in South Florida, a gun was a most reasonable acquisition to make.

He had been living in Ft. Lauderdale for just over a year, and the place made him nervous. There were days when he could walk down certain streets (he did not have the protection of a car to get around) with the sense that a third of the people he saw had something wrong with them—of a mental or criminal nature.

The week before Christmas last year, when shopping was at its peak, they had closed the Galleria Mall for a day because of bomb threats. Last spring, 170 convicted murderers and rapists were released from jails in the Ft. Lauderdale area—something to do with screwups in their trials and overcrowding in the prisons. There was not just a lot of homeless people on the streets (many just financially unfortunate), there was a plethora of people in need of psychiatric help who had nowhere to go. The city had absolutely no concern for the mentally ill. If a citizen cracked up and made a public disturbance, he was thrown into jail.

Rick found the unstable ones easily recognizable by their eyes, which seemed to be in a state of petrification. Eyes wide open in the glare of a tropical sun. Hard, marbled whites centered by unwavering pupils that looked at everything and everyone in their path with the intensity of a laser beam. Eyes within faces that were not tanned, but burned—skin like hides left for too long in a boiling sun.

He had listened to a man on a bus one day tell another man— who was obviously a stranger—how he had recently had to shoot someone. He had gone to a check-cashing store, and after he had returned outside, a man had demanded his money. The thief did not have a gun, but he was a large man and he looked menacing. "Fuckin' wayyy out there" was the description the victim used.

And so the victim had shot the thief in the leg. Said he had learned long ago to always carry a gun whenever he was going to cash a check.

The trouble with what otherwise would have been a story about obvious self-defense was the demeanor of the victim. For he had those petrified eyes—an intensely focused (upon the stranger) beam of hatred emanating from a blackened face. And as he told of his encounter, with growing agitation, his hand gripped the bulge of what looked to be a gun in the pocket of his mud-splattered green fatigues.

Rick wondered, when he watched the local news, why there were so many people living in the area who went around stealing dogs and cats just for the purpose of torture.

Everyone he knew had a drug-pusher story because dealers in South Florida were as evident as insects. And so he would tell people of his first few months in his Victoria Park apartment, when once or twice a week the same two men would knock on his door in the middle of the night. Rick would look at them through the peephole without ever opening the door and explain to the men, in the same way every time they came, that the former tenant was no longer residing in the apartment. The men would offer to him the sale of cocaine anyway, and he would say, "No thank you," as though turning down a proposition for Girl Scout cookies. He was afraid to tell the police, and he was astounded by brains so far gone that they made the same mistake every week.

He worked in an area of the beach that was full of hotels. Two blocks down from the hotel in which he worked as a banquet waiter there had been a murder in another hotel kitchen (just two weeks before he bought the gun). A supervisor had cut an employee's hours. The employee had gone home and then returned to the hotel a little later to shoot the supervisor to death. Days later, a dishwasher had an argument with his supervisor in the kitchen of a Key West hotel. The dishwasher was accused of placing forks in the containers reserved for spoons. He quit the job and he, too, went home to fetch a gun to return to the kitchen where he blew away the supervisor and a few other workers as well.

Around this time, Rick noticed a sign had gone up on the wall of the Human Resources office in his own hotel of employment. Instructions on how to "dismiss personnel." Safety measures for supervisors who fired workers. Although the instructions had to do with carrying out the dismissal in a calm manner, Rick imagined that, from now on, a supervisor would not whisper words of expulsion without first pointing a gun at the employee's head.

He was amused by an article he had read in the paper that told of depression in the ranks of the employees at the hotel where the first murder had taken place. The hotel had called in professionals to help the employees cope with the tragedy. He imagined a sign going up in the Human Resources office of that hotel— SHIT HAPPENS.

One evening, Rick heard a banquet manager say that he thought certain members of the staff were growing increasingly hostile. He wondered if any of them carried guns. And then a week later, this same manager was fired for stealing bar receipts. But the staff, when they heard the news, were bitter at the reason for the manager's dismissal because they had long suspected him of stealing their tips that were left with him by clients. They had complained to Human Resources, and yet their action was not among the reasons for the manager's dismissal. But it most definitely was among the reasons why the manager worried about having his head blown off by one of the waiters.

So this was the emotional and criminal climate of where Rick lived and worked. Ft. Lauderdale—where the sounds of ambulances and police cars screamed all night long. Where guns were so notoriously easy to come by that people came down from the North for that very reason. And so finally he had decided to buy his own handgun. Through legal channels. A .38 Special snub-nose revolver. Mostly because of the rednecks who called him "cocksucker."

Rick was thirty-six years old. He was homosexual, and so far as homophobic reaction to his appearance, he could not be described as effeminate. He took a bus to work and liked to walk the two miles home every night. He had been doing this for no more than a few days when one night around 11 p.m. a car passed him on the way home, with faces hung out of the windows screaming "cocksucker." The same thing would happen a few times a week. Though it was never the same car, the voices all screamed variations on the word "cocksucker." The faces hanging out of the windows may have been different with every incident, but they were always young and white and frequently had Southern accents. And when they slowed as they passed, the faces seemed insane; they were so violently red and he could see the veins popping out on their temples as though they were all on the verge of strokes.

In his calmer moments, he wondered why they had such an obsession with cocksucking. But at the time of the occurrences, he was always scared and, increasingly, very angry. And he refused to give up his nightly walks.

Saturday night was the big bar night on the beach when traffic stretched bumper to bumper along A1A, which was the route he took to walk home. On a hot, humid Saturday night at the end of May, he had his worst experience with the homophobic rednecks. And it was excruciating because the abuse lasted for so long in the stalled traffic. The car inched along beside him as he walked, and one drunken face red with rage hung out of the front window— two out of the back. The one in the front did most of the screaming while the two in back egged him on and sometimes contributed.

"Hey, faggot, wanna suck my cock? I got a big juicy one here for yuh. Come on, faggot! I'll letcha suck it for just fifty dollars. Come on, you fucking faggot! You can suck it and then I can shoot your fucking brains out!" And so on for about ten minutes, with cars in front and back for an audience. And no one was any help at all. Not a cop in sight. The three short-haired kids screamed. Rick wondered if they would try to force him into the car, and he realized that if he could have anything in the world during those long minutes, it would have been a gun to end their miserable lives.

At first, after he had bought the gun, it made him nervous just to hold it in his hand. He pictured himself clumsily tripping the trigger and somehow shooting himself. Though the weather was hot now in late spring, he took to wearing thick baggy pants just so he could carry the gun in his pocket without being too obvious. Yet he made sure there was something of a bulge so that any prospective assailant would notice. Not knowing what to do with the gun inside the hotel, where he wore the thin material of tuxedo pants, he decided to take a chance and keep it in his locker. But lockers were frequently robbed by the employees, and so after a few days, he finally bought a holster to strap around the calf of his right leg. This way, he told himself with a smile, he was always ready to react if he ever got fired.

The staff at the hotel were mostly Latin Americans. Rick was one of six American men, and half of them were gay. How many of the Latinos were gay, he could only guess because Latin American men seemed cautious if their preference was same sex. But Rick and the other two American gay men were open about themselves in conversations during work—they did not whisper. Everyone on the staff—he was sure—was aware of their identities, including the Cuban banquet manager who made it obvious that he thought of them as ridiculous human beings. He was not hostile, but he toyed with gay men. To him, they were women sporting dicks. He was careful not to do or say anything that could be construed as discriminatory (and so cause a complaint to be filed). But there was always a smirk on his face when he spoke to the gay men, and sometimes he used a falsetto voice or mimicked effeminacy. Rick hated him.

Carrying the gun around with him at work and everywhere else he went became a pleasurable experience after he got over his initial nervousness. He was willing to bet that there were not many other gay men who carried guns, and why, he could not imagine. Every gay person *needed* to carry a gun because there were so many fanatics in society who truly hated homosexuals and wanted them dead. It was the one hatred that crossed all lines. In every religion and race there were people who hated homosexuals. Thus, a gun was a requirement for survival in a world of insanity that was getting sicker with each passing year.

   Rick felt free of tension and fear for the first time since he had
moved from Boston to South Florida. The gun strapped to his
leg had the same effect on his bearing as cocaine had had in
his younger days—he felt safe within the high of superiority. And
he knew that he emanated this newfound image of the indomitable
man. He walked aggressively now, and he looked everyone in the
eyes, including the myriad of unsavory characters who were loose
on the streets of Ft. Lauderdale. He used to look anywhere but in
their vicinity for fear of inviting attack. Anymore, he not only
looked directly into their eyes, he also sent the telepathic message
that he would blow their fucking faces off if they even so much as
tried to bum a cigarette from him.
   Of course, he had no intention of actually using the gun. In spite
of knowing that he was not up to the task of defending himself in
case of attack, he had never in his life been a victim of physical
violence—which he thought of as the only circumstance that justi-
fied the use of a gun. What he felt these days was a vast relief, a
holiday from fear. He played in his mind with the thought of what
he could do to anyone who would harm him. And this helped to
make up for past verbal assaults. It was the power that thrilled him
and not any intention to really use that power.
   There were times when he could feel ridiculous about the way
in which the gun had changed his attitude. He knew he had
become something of an American cliché. For instance, there
were occasions when walking down a street he would become
conscious of the gun against his leg and this would cause an
erection. And he would think of himself as a cartoon American
superbutch ready to draw his pistol. Looking provocatively into
the eyes of desperado types he passed on the street, he sent out
his message of destruction while feeling the erection harden. He
was a lethal flirt.

   One unjust aspect of his life remained.
   After the manager who had been stealing tips and bar receipts
had been fired, the banquet staff's paychecks continued to be

devoid of tips that they knew had been left for them by the clients who paid for the various functions.

Rick, and most of his co-workers, suspected the sneaky homophobe whom Rick hated. His name was Carlos, and since he was the banquet manager, he was the top man in the banquet department. And since their complaints of theft against a lower-level manager had failed to produce results (until the hotel owners themselves believed they were being ripped off), the frustrated waiters lacked hope in making a case against Carlos.

Another factor that prevented the waiters from filing complaints against Carlos was the nature of their position in the hotel's employee structure. Banquet waiters had no set schedules and worked at the discretion of the banquet manager who scheduled people in accordance with the amount of functions to be held in a given week. There were always more banquet staff on call then there was work, and so Carlos had much room to play favorites. File a complaint against him in Human Resources (which would take months to investigate) and your hours were sure to be cut. And so a maddening situation existed. People felt certain that they worked for a thief who took money out of their paychecks and who was safe in his activities from a hotel ownership that had already proven how little they cared about employee complaints.

Signs of employee disenchantment began to proliferate inside the hotel, and Rick was glad about every rebellious act he heard of. He was very bitter about the money he was deprived of each week. He applauded the employees who were stealing from the supply rooms, and he thought it was no wonder that guest rooms were being entered and stolen from with outrageous frequency.

Graffiti communicating grievances against management spread from employee rest rooms to the walls of the corridors in the work areas. And then the messages began to appear on the walls of the guest elevators. "This hotel exploits poor people." "This hotel steals from the workers' paychecks." "The management sucks each other's dicks." (And Rick's mind lingered over the last message, thinking of the rednecks' obsession and how the accusation was—in the brain of the writer—one of the worst conceivable. But now as he mulled all of this over, he felt the gun against his leg and experienced for the first time in his life the sexual glow of the abominated outlaw who carries a gun in defense of his deeds.)

As the workers began to turn themselves into criminals because of corrupt management, the banquet manager became proportionately more insulting to the waiters. And at one meeting where Carlos presided, he had a most disquieting effect on Rick's nerves.

Carlos stood in front of twenty waiters and waitresses wearing a beautifully tailored suit. He was forty years old, and on his slender frame there was the bulge of an indulged stomach. His hair was dyed black, and in the time that Rick had been at the hotel, Carlos had had cosmetic work done around his eyes. As always, he stood perfectly composed in front of the group (a demeanor he had developed especially for the hotel's clients who spent tens of thousands of dollars on most dinner parties). He spoke softly, with his hands of perfectly manicured nails folded in front of him. And his topic of discussion for the waiters was piss.

"We have people on the staff who are pissing on the floor in areas of the hotel. I do not believe that I am talking to you today about this repulsive subject. But I have been instructed to tell you that anyone caught pissing in the corridors or the elevators will be fired immediately. Because of the obvious discontent among the servers lately, they are the employees whom we are most suspicious of."

The staff stared at him, bearing rock-hard expressions of anger. Carlos looked at the floor, shifted his feet nervously. And then as though to crack a joke that would put everyone else in the room at ease, he smiled at Rick and the other two gay men who all sat together. He said, "You guys aren't going in for water sports with each other in the elevators, are you?"

To Rick, the words were just another way of calling him a cocksucker. Like the rednecks in the passing cars. And he reached down and pressed his hand against the outline of the gun strapped to his leg. He said to Carlos, "I thought Human Resources had instructed the managers on how to behave with employees ever since the shootings in the other hotels."

When the schedule for the following week went up on the bulletin board, he found that his hours had been cut in half.

There was a young black Haitian man standing next to him in front of the board, and Rick said to him, "You know, Yves, if we all got together, we could bring that motherfucker Carlos down. He can't cut the hours for all of us. Who'd work the functions? He's stealing our money and he uses the schedule to keep us in line."

Yves looked like he felt sorry for him. In a low voice, so no passerby would hear, he said, "Oh, man, you can't get any of these people together. This is a multicultural group. Among the Latinos, the people who came from one country south of the border don't like the people who come from another country south of the border. And it's not just that the blacks don't get along with the whites; the blacks don't even get along with each other. I know the American blacks don't like it that I'm in this country. And among you whites, so many are hung up on hating the Jews and nobody likes the gays except the gays themselves. No man. You can just forget about getting these people together. And by the way, when was it you started carrying a gun? I caught a glimpse one day when you were relaxing in the cafeteria. You had your legs stretched out under the table and I know I saw a strap to a holster."

"I've had it a couple of weeks now."

"Smart move. You need one. I've just about decided to carry one too. Fuckin' Florida's crazy, man. I thought I'd get a little peace when I left Haiti. I tell you, I came home one night last month and found all my valuables gone outta my apartment. I've had it, man. Third time in the last year. I'm gonna get a gun, and if I ever find out who ripped me off, I'm gonna blow their fuckin' brains out."

After work that night he walked home and decided that he was sick of living in Florida. He did not belong in this warring, scam-riddled state. He felt preposterous because it was so hot out and yet he walked home wearing long pants just because of the gun strapped to his leg. He was already losing all sense of adventure and power. The gun was probably a mistake. If you lived in a place where a gun was a necessity, then that place was not worth living in. Besides, down here there were just too many temptations to use the gun.

He decided that he would give his two-week notice. And then pack up and go back to Boston.

Late the next morning, he rode his bike to the bank where he cashed his checks. He always used the bike for this errand so that he could make a speedy getaway with the cash.

While entering the parking lot, he passed four black men leaning against the back of a truck. One of them said to him, "Hey, gimme a cigarette, man." Rick answered, "I don't smoke," even though he knew they could see the pack in his shirt pocket.

He had already gone by them when he heard one of them erupt—"Motherfucker!"

Rick's first reaction was that the guy was crazy because this was a white neighborhood. Also, the Ft. Lauderdale police were thought to be racist (according to the blacks) and never needed much of an excuse to pick up a black man.

"Your fuckin' mother sucks black dick. You know that, man?"

This came from one of the other four, and Rick was disoriented because he could not understand why they would take this chance. And as he pulled up in front of the bank and noticed that some of the cars in front had white men and women inside, he grew panicky. How could the blacks do this? And he took the bike off to the side of the building where they kept a bike rack. As he bent down to lock the bike, he heard a third voice.

"Fuckin' mother takes all the black dick she can take! You hear me, motherfucker?"

He stepped over to the wall of the bank where he was not visible from the lot and took the gun from the holster, putting it in his pocket. When he got inside the bank, he would tell security to call the police.

But when he walked around to the entrance, the truck was pulling out of the lot. As he pushed through the door and into the bank, a middle-aged man in a business suit walked behind him and said, "Getting worse down here all the time."

Because the blacks had left the lot, he decided not to tell security. But as he stepped up to the teller's window to sign the check, he could not control the trembling of his hands. The teller, a young woman with a pinched look to her face that said, "Don't bother me," looked at him curiously before reinstating the no-nonsense visage.

Again he thought of reporting the incident, but the cold air of indifference on the teller's face decided for him. He calmed himself with the reminder that his days in South Florida were nearly over and he took the cash and left the bank.

He walked back around the side of the bank to the rack, and with his panic having retreated, a space was left inside him where hatred came to call. He had never had anything against blacks. He had never talked against them. He was not a racist. And now it turned out that these niggers were no better than the rednecks said they were. He willed that the truck somehow got demolished on the highway, and he pictured the four of them ripped apart and bleeding to death and no one stopping to help.

Lost in thoughts of retribution, he knelt to unlock the bike—taking the chain and slamming it against the walk, which was the face of the one who had asked for the cigarette. Then he suddenly became aware of shoes to the side, over against the wall.

"Hand it over, motherfucker! Fast!"

It was as though the force of the chain against the walk had released the presence of the man who stood against the wall. Out of sight from the parking lot. With an empty field behind and the Intracoastal across from the side of the bank. They were alone together.

He was not holding a gun on him, and when the man said, "Fast, motherfucker! Take me ten seconds to twist your ugly face outta shape for life," Rick knew he had no gun to pull. He figured Rick for a pushover.

On his knees, Rick took the cash from his pocket and began to rise, but the man said, "You just stay down on your knees and hand it to me." And he did as he was told.

With the money in his hand, the black was grinning. "That look like a natural position to you down there. I'll bet you a cocksucker. Am I right? You a cocksucker, boy?"

Rick stared up at him—said nothing.

"Empty out your pockets. Maybe you got a little more."

Rick smiled up at the man. A great big broad smile that would have been construed as full of love by anyone else who happened to be present. And with possibly the most graceful move of his life, he took the gun from his pocket, which felt like it was of silk material the piece slid out so easily and quickly.

The black man took the first hit in the chest with a look of great astonishment on his face. He was against the wall anyway, and his knees buckled and he slid down the wall, but just a few feet. He was a big strong man and he seemed to revive from the hole in his chest in seconds. He had both hands covering the hole and blood was running out over his hands.

He attempted to speak but the wind had been knocked out of him, and he was trying hard to swallow and get air and speak all at the same time.

Rick was standing now, pointing the gun at the man's face and transfixed by the Adam's apple that seemed to be struggling to leave the man's throat. He was relaxed and as happy as he had ever been in his life, and he decided to shoot the Adam's apple out of the man's throat. He lowered the gun and took aim and squeezed the trigger and watched with sheer exhilaration as the throat exploded in blood and the assailant slid down the wall into a sitting position. With no throat. Just a head—a face hanging down and only the top half of the face visible as the blood gushed from the mouth and from what used to be a throat. And the only thought Rick had in his mind as he stood there looking at this mess was that it was truly disgusting how much big niggers bled.

He lost all sense of time.

But at some point, he was surrounded by bank customers who had been in the parking lot, and police. The black man had already been taken away in an ambulance. Slowly the buzz of voices and the questions of the police got through to him and he became aware that he was a hero. So many of the white faces claimed to have seen the black man go around the back of the bank to rob Rick. So many said they had witnessed the first encounter and all the name-calling—which surprised Rick. He had not realized that there had been so many people parked in the lot.

And the police were going to take him to the station, but they seemed apologetic and assured him that his was obviously a case of self-defense.

He was just about to get into the police car when a young man came up beside him. He had very short blond hair. His face was bright red and his eyes were electric with excitement. He said to Rick, "Congratulations, man! You really nailed that cocksucker!"

As he rode away with the police, Rick had the thought that he would change his plans. He would not return to Boston.

After the business of the shooting was over with, he would not leave town. He knew for certain that there was definitely a place for him right here in South Florida.

A Refugee from the Ocean

All he ever knew growing up were the fields. Grain. The flat boredom of the Midwest, where the only poetic variations of nature eased and flashed across the unobstructed view of the sky.

There were farm boys and girls who lived out there who could conceive of no other place to live—no other way to live. But he knew from his first viewing of a film featuring an ocean that he had been born in the wrong place. He must have seemed a strange boy to anyone who observed him. Always looking up—always lost in the colors of the sky in order to forget about the fields.

His inner world felt like a barren field that had gone too long without rain. He suffered from a mystical dehydration. By the time he was eighteen, he walked around with the sense that he had been deprived of eighteen years of living. He felt flattened and drained of juice, like the slain fields in times of harvest.

Even though he was aware of his forbidden attraction to boys, the erotic effect was dreamlike. The tedium of those squared-off fields reacted on him as though he had been sprayed by a sexual pest control. Stimulation was impossible to sustain within an environment so devoid of variation and sensuality. Seeds of imaginative possibility would sprout in his desperate mind at the sight of a good-looking farm boy, only to wither on the vine of his ripening body as the vast fields swallowed his lusty vision.

He read a lot in high school and fell in love with the plays of Eugene O'Neill who was so drawn to the sea. He read a biography of the playwright and learned of the place where his plays were first performed. A town in the east where artists and writers lived by the ocean—Provincetown on Cape Cod.

He did not know that homosexuals lived in Provincetown (O'Neill was straight and did not write of homosexuals), and yet

he instinctively speculated that there might be a connection between the ocean, artists, and his own burgeoning sexual nature. It
could be the ocean that would ignite the dynamics of his sex, and
it could be that a population of artists would understand him (or
at least not condemn). But somehow it was the ocean with its
teeming evidence of the food chain that excited him. He associated the endless strokes of the tides that nibbled away coastlines
with masculine sex. The ocean's raw power was a masculine
power. The ocean was cruel and insatiable. The life of the ocean
fed upon itself and ravished the land. And he did not know how
the idea was born inside him, but he thought that sexual affairs
with men had to be thrilling orgasmic contests of usurpation. If
the relationship was good, both partners digested each other until
they became one—with the power of two. If the relationship was
bad (one not strong enough for the other), then one man went
away greatly nourished while the other was left barren.

   At nineteen, he hitchhiked to the New England Coast. And it
seemed to fit his vision of the ocean as a voracious sexual power
when he found Provincetown to be so small, way out on the tip of
the Cape, as though wasting away in the surrounding ocean.

   Beyond the town were two beaches—Herring Cove on the bay
side and Race Point on the Atlantic Ocean. Seeking information
about how to find O'Neill's house on Race Point, he learned that
the ocean had taken the house a long time ago. Walking down
Commercial Street, the main street in Provincetown, he could see
a sandbar across the bay (Cape Cod Bay) that was called Long
Point, and it reminded him of an elusive eel as it slithered off the
hook of the Cape. And as he walked, intoxicated by a headful of
cool sea breeze, he knew that certain men were looking at him in
a way he had never before experienced. And these admiring
glances flowed together with the aroma of clams that wafted
from kitchens, and an effeminate buoyancy he noticed in the step
of individual boys his own age, and sixties music cascading out
from bars—psychedelic music (not popular where he came from)
that had the effect of making the town seem even smaller, while
he himself felt blown out larger from exhilaration as his eyes
drifted from the searchlight look of men and boys out to the

slithering eel of Long Point. It was all so intense and such a shock to his upbringing.

His bursting newcomer's head, so inundated with provocation and possibilities, would most probably have suffered a stroke had he known of the stealthy activities surrounding him when he viewed the ocean from the dunes of Race Point. But it was his first day in Provincetown and his first sweeping view of the ocean, and he was transfixed. While his soul soared out over the ocean and the bay, his future lay waiting below in the hollows and falls of the wild dunes where armies of men (but only a few girls at that time) were making love. He did not see them on that day in early June as they lay in thickets and coves, hiding from the park rangers, but the dunes would come to mean the most naturally erotic setting for sex he would ever know in his life. Primordial coupling near the shore of the always-fucking sea. The bedroom of sand. As close a return to original sex as anyone could know.

He just stood there on top of the dune with his mouth hanging open, so stricken was he by the magnificent ocean. Stood there in his farm boy bib overalls that he would soon learn to wear without shirt or underwear and had absolutely no inkling of what was going on just down the slopes that surrounded him. How could he know, when queer sex was forbidden sex whose price was an eternity of roasting flesh in hell?

Oh, man! All that water! His eyes took in that point where the bay converged with the ocean in a smash of white foam currents, and he was mesmerized. Such incredible power! What enormous force! And even out to the east where the water was relatively calm, the inherent muscle was obvious.

He felt an infantile frustration because there was no way he could actually get inside this body he had fallen in love with. How could he ever connect with water the way he wanted to connect, which was sexually? He had a quick fantasy of swimming nude and jerking off into the ocean and then thought of how insignificant it would make him feel. And he laughed. To shoot a load into the ocean was like watering fields in the rain. Who needed you?

He stood there so astonished and frustrated and yet feeling wildly free. A hard-on bulged from his overalls as he looked all around and up in the sky for planes, and then he peeled off his clothes and let himself roll down the dune to the bottom where, filled with aromas of the sea that smelled like cum, he lay on his back and jerked off amid the men fucking like foxes in the surrounding garden of sand. Unaware of how his privacy had been respected by his newfound neighbors—the hornball gentlemen of New England.

It wasn't so expensive to rent a small cottage on the bay back in the sixties (the oceanside was government-protected land). During his first week in Provincetown, he kept to himself. He would sit outside on the steps of his one-room shack, or he would ride the used bike he had bought out to Race Point to look out over the manic-depressive ocean.

He had never drunk alcohol back home, but now he began to indulge—alone and sitting on the cottage steps. It seemed appropriate that he would ease his loneliness with liquids. After all, his whole existence was liquids now as he sat between bay and ocean and felt so totally centered by water. And he knew that there was another reason to drink—to dredge up the courage to confront all those strange men and boys he had seen in town.

He checked out a book about Provincetown from the library, and his reading confirmed a sense of destiny in having chosen this spot—so far from home—in which to live. He actually compared himself physically to the shape of the land. Just as he knew that people saw him as rather thin and frail, he knew he was, in fact, much stronger than they thought. And although Provincetown was only three miles wide and caught between two bodies of water, he was delighted to read that the town was an ecological receiver. Although Provincetown looked like it could disappear next year, it was the first third of Cape Cod jutting out from the mainland that was eroding, and the currents were carrying the sand out to the tip of the Cape. Someday a good part of the Cape would no longer exist, but a fattened Provincetown would remain as an island of its own (instead of being part of a peninsula).

And then there were the stay-at-home pirates who once inhabited the land. They built fortunes by being receivers. They were scavengers who would wait for ships bearing cargoes of treasure to crash on the shoals around Long Point and then they would go out and loot the ships. And their ancestors also waited for prey in the sixties, as each summer they took the tourists for all they were worth.

He identified with all that he read. The deceptive look of fading away only to be nourished by sea and so made stronger. And, sitting on the steps watching the bay, he even had intimations of himself as looter, for he had learned just how much of a booming tourist town Provincetown had become. And out of all the people who would come here, it served to reason that many came because of the strange men who lived here. Of which he was one. And once he screwed his courage up, there would not be enough locals to satisfy his misleading quiet and shy personality. It would be the new infusion of strange men who came and went and then were replaced by others whom he would be waiting for. To make up for the years in the Midwest when he had not lived.

One night, sitting on the steps, high in flights of animalist fantasy bordered by ocean and sex, he finally left the cottage and strode purposefully into town—as though on the way to a competition.

Later that night, he left the Atlantic House with a boy his own age and proposed that they go out to the beach instead of returning to one of their cottages. And once they were on the dark shore of Race Point, near the tide that was gently slapping the shore, all shyness vanished in the excitement of his one wish— which was to drain the ocean out of his prey. And there was never any of the doubt and competitiveness of two young men who were not yet certain of their sexual positions. He never gave the boy time to think. And the boy, in return, seemed happy to be a predator's late-night snack.

He vowed he would never leave Provincetown, and during his first full year out there, especially in summer, he felt as though descended from those scavenging pirates of old. The bars were ships stranded on the shoals of the Cape and he went out nightly to loot, but differed from his spiritual ancestors in that it was the crew he would make off with and not the treasure.

He was so ecstatic to have found, on one small plot of land, so many who were like himself that through the summer he never really felt the distinctions of the individual. Never related to a person but instead to a collection.

And in winter, even his few short affairs did not register knowledge of a particular man. For one thing, it was cold weather and sparse population that promoted these affairs. It was quite simply easier to share a cottage with someone than to freeze walking to a bar every night where he would only suffer the reminder that he had already had the cream of the crop anyway.

Aside from nature lovers, the reason why the sea town gays and bisexuals stayed in winter was because drinking oneself senseless was not such an unpardonable offense as it would be on the mainland. And they moved in with each other for economic reasons—paying only half the rent left more money to drink.

He quit drinking that winter because the devastating effects of alcoholism were all around him. He lived for a while with one young man who drank day and night and was always afraid to be alone. He said that living in a place surrounded by water caused him to think of death constantly. He said the ocean was too much of a reminder of his own transience. And yet he would not leave. He said he loved the ocean too much to leave.

He knew what the young man meant, in a way. He was beginning to think that his own oversexed way of living might have something to do with a love of the eternal ocean that left him feeling insignificant. Could it be that he fucked so much just to realize his own life?

He thought about erosion, about pounding waves that took away the land he lived on. Even out there in Provincetown, the ecological receiver, he knew that at least parts of the beaches were being washed to the sea. And sometimes he was haunted by the thought of eroding some part of the men he fucked with. The Cape, the men he knew—all draining away, eroding, dying. And when he scolded himself for being pretentious, another part of him would counter with the idea that maybe pretentiousness was a necessary antidote for the sad business of being alive.

A year passed; he turned twenty years old. During the slow time of his life by the ocean, he had become even more mesmerized or hypnotized by the moods of the sea. He could stare for hours now at the ocean or the bay without a thought in his head. And it was this addiction that formed his alliance with Stewart.

Stewart was exactly twice his age. He came from Canada where he had been the curator at a museum. But he came from a wealthy family and had decided upon an early retirement in Provincetown. He lived on a large inheritance. He could afford to do nothing, and that is what he did.

He bought a large house that was located on a hill and had a sweeping view of the bay. He would sit for hours on his patio and drink vodka and look out over the bay. He was a distinguished-looking man, tall and slender with silver hair. He smoked a pipe and switched from vodka to expensive scotch after five in the evening. He held his liquor well, and it was only obvious that he was high late at night when he slurred just a bit.

The young man from the Midwest went home with him one night, and after indifferent sex they woke the next morning to find their true compatibility. They could sit together on the patio for hours staring at the bay, and without the slightest trace of unease, neither would say a word to the other.

He half moved in with Stewart, which is to say that he continued to pay rent on his cottage in order to retain a getaway. Stewart liked to drink and he did not. Stewart really did not care about sex and he did. And yet he loved being with Stewart. He loved the calmness of the man and the hours they spent together in silence. And Stewart obviously appreciated his company, too, for he stopped going to bars. In fact, there came a point where the only human being Stewart would have contact with was his "half" housemate.

This relationship had been going on for a year when one summer evening, Stewart broke from his trance-sitting on the patio. He turned to the young man sitting next to him and said, "I think you should apply to a college in Boston. I'll pay for your education—your needs. You can come out here on weekends."

The young man looked over at him and wondered if this was a first—Stewart drunk at five. Lately it had seemed that Stewart was not holding up so well under all his drinking. But Stewart leaned even closer to his chair, and he was not slurring when he looked into his eyes and said, "I remember you told me how much you hated the Midwest. And I know that you think this is where you belong. But . . . fields of grain . . . vistas of sea. In a way, they can have the same effect. You are becoming hollowed into a husk."

He looked into Stewart's eyes for a full minute, and Stewart returned this probe with expressions that seemed to slide back and forth between profundity and amusement. But when it became apparent that Stewart had nothing more to add in the way of a retraction, the young man rose from his chair and left the patio—left the house entirely. He returned to his cottage and did not see Stewart again for weeks.

He lived within a troubled mind for the first time since he had left the Midwest. In fact, he was filled with the dread of having to leave the ocean. He knew his time on the Cape was over for at least some four years because he trusted Stewart. He knew he would do what Stewart told him to do because the older man advised with a detached pragmatism that was so much like the way the younger man reasoned. And there was the fact that the advice came at Stewart's own expense. The young man knew he was all Stewart had in the way of companionship. This offer of a way into the real world severed Stewart's lifeline to anything except the sea. And it was impossible that Stewart would wish for total ocean solitude—wasn't it?

Possessed of sexual juices that never ran dry, he did not see himself as a "husk." He entered Boston University in the fall out of what he thought of as a respect for a wisdom that was derived from Stewart's meditations by the sea. And, of course, he could return within a short time if the wisdom proved to be misguided. He was doing a friend a favor by taking him up on his advice. He would give college a try, but he really did not think he would last long.

He was immediately overwhelmed by great surprise in his new life. Boston in the late sixties. Essentially a conservative city in behavioral attitudes, it was, in 1968, undergoing the same tumultuous questioning of American values as the rest of the country. Every student he came in contact with seemed to be rebelling against something. Every student had a cause. The campus was a hotbed of unrest.

At first, he was a titillated observer, but when he found he had to deal with a draft board and its consequent issue of Vietnam, the cumulative ignorance of his short adult life became apparent. For out in Provincetown, he had never thought once of being at risk during those times when he heard or read the word Vietnam.

So his introduction into what was going on in the United States brought about immediate involvement with the issues just because he learned quickly that his own personal survival was at stake. And he learned how no issue was simple—every patch torn in the quilt of American society unraveled some other patch. For example, he learned it was possible to escape the military through student deferment, but by taking that route, he was helping to place in danger the lives of the poor and the minorities who would go in his place. And so he asked himself if it would be a more honorable exemption if he were to declare himself as homosexual to the draft board. Taking that position would be to side with a minority group and yet still have the effect of escaping the draft. But then he would get confused because intuition told him that you could not be calculating and moral at the same time. And besides, what would a homosexual deferment do to his chances of success in the world? Wasn't he tarring and feathering himself? In disgust, he got a student deferment because of the pressure to decide right away and his inability to come to grips with the confusion of a society lost in a quagmire of self-doubt.

But there were times of exhilaration too. Gay rights was on the move, and even though he would not declare his sexual identity to the draft board, he was happy to march in the streets for equality. It felt sexual to be a revolutionary. And there was a heightened awareness to the sex he had with the other activists. Some nights he would go to bed with a boy all fired up with the thought that they could both be shot to death during the next day's protest. And the fucking would be the most intense he had ever known.

And there were drugs and The Beatles and the angry aftermath of assassinations. And boys with long hair and clothes that made boys and girls look deliciously alike. And he even found that he was scholastically bright. Learning came easy to him, and there was so very much to learn. And experience.

He would, at first, visit Stewart every week, even if it was just for a few hours. But oh, God, the man was hard to take after the week of activity in Boston. Stewart had so little to say as the young man gushed with the details of the previous week and then waited in vain for a reaction.

All Stewart wanted to do—as the country went up in flames— was stare out to sea.

Not that the young student had forgotten how beautiful life by the ocean actually was. He had plans to someday own a house in Provincetown. His soul was with the ocean. He would definitely return to live there for at least whole summers. But there was another world too, and he could not for the life of him get Stewart to acknowledge that fact.

Winter came, and he found it too boring for words whenever he went out to Provincetown. And so he began to skip weekends with the rationalization that Stewart would not even notice his absence. The man seemed physically smaller, more diminished, every time he went out to see him. He was only in his early forties, but he moved like a man of eighty. There were times when the young man came through the door and out to the patio, where he knew he would find Stewart all bundled up in his chair, and Stewart did not seem to recognize who he was. He looked at the young man passively, as though he were a friendly but anonymous apparition.

But he never had to remind Stewart of money. Stewart never forgot to send the checks that paid for the young man's needs in Boston—and everything else he wanted too.

He had been in Boston for nearly four years when he suffered a crisis of dissatisfaction with every aspect of his life. The country, in the seventies, had entered into a mood of moral rigidity that made him wonder what the great upheaval of the sixties had really been all about. The gay rights movement now seemed adverse to his real sexual personality. He missed the outlaw image of the sexual deviant; he did not want to be brought into the mainstream of society. Society was boring and sex was boring, too, when it struggled to be sanctioned. He doubted seriously that he could ever be happy in a lover relationship. There was something restless inside him that prevented day-to-day living with one man.

He was preparing to enter law school in the fall, and he wondered how it had happened that he had chosen law for a career when he had no respect for the law whatsoever. It was a joke to believe there was such a thing as justice in the courts. On the scales that weighed the arguments for any given case of import, money tipped the balance. The name of the game was to represent the clients who had a lot of money. The thought of practicing law bored him to death. It would be more fun for a nice-looking young man like himself to make his fortune sucking rich dick.

In his discouragement, a longing for the past occupied his thoughts through most of the days. He missed being nineteen years old. He had led a life of poetic naturalism in Provincetown, with his equation of the ocean and male sex as one. And he missed that first year with Stewart who knew the art of silent reverence for the sea. Stewart had been wrong to send him away. And now look at the two of them. Stewart was nearly an imbecile and he felt drained of life. He was becoming the husk Stewart claimed him to be years ago back in Provincetown. But Stewart had been wrong; his time by the sea had been his pure time, and all Boston had done for him was to prepare the way for a life of hollow tedium.

And it was at this time that the news of Stewart's death came to him. A heart attack.

He had never even known that Stewart had had heart trouble. And now he felt free to go ahead and implement the plan he had been hoping to act upon. He wanted to go back to Provincetown and live, but the thought of confronting Stewart had caused a failure of nerves. Why, he did not know.

After all, Stewart had been out of it for years. Stewart had been incapable of judging him, of pointing out the great waste of money and time involved with the young man's turnabout. He could not figure out why he had hesitated in facing the invalid. And by the way, since he was an invalid, he could have made his days easier. He could have taken care of him.

But none of his reasoning had allowed him to go out to Provincetown and announce his decision. The thought of standing there on the patio in front of the silent man whose eyes would remain on the sea . . . the thought of telling him he wanted to return . . .

Stewart's death not only removed the obstacle of confrontation, it had placed the young man right at that point in time where desire and fate acquiesce to each other. He had no doubt that

Stewart had not only left him a sizable amount of money but the house also.

On an Indian summer day in late September, the young man stood on the patio of Stewart's house. Late September is the most enchanting of times on Cape Cod, and the weather was warm and the leaves of the trees a sweetly sad brown-red and gold. From the patio, the bay appeared too calm and peaceful to move. Although move it always did.

He was there with Stewart's doctor who was one of the few people who saw Stewart during his last years. He had been asked by Stewart's lawyer to help the young man in packing up the house. Stewart's sister had requested that they do this as a favor before her arrival. For she was to be the new mistress of the house.

The doctor—a man known to drink only a trifle less than the alcoholics he treated—sat in Stewart's chair. He was small, prematurely aged at fifty, and in fact had a bit of a buzz on as he talked about his ex-patient. "He couldn't stand that damn sister of his. She's a spinster or a dyke; I don't know which. But she'd come down from Toronto from time to time in the last few years, and she was crazy about Provincetown. Probably found it easier to get her twat licked here as opposed to Toronto. I'm surprised he gave her the house, the way he went on about her to me. Back when he still bothered to talk, that is. Anyway, I would have thought the house would have gone to you."

He was dazed by the outcome of the will. It had come as a shock even though he had inherited a substantial amount of money. He knew, as he had listened to the lawyer, that Stewart's act had been a symbolic one. But he had been so sure, before coming out to Provincetown, that once he arrived he would not leave again. Now, listening to the doctor, everything seemed at odds.

The doctor was studying his face and he asked, "How long did you know Stewart?"

"Close to five years."

"Did he say much about his heart condition?"

"He never said a word."

The young man did not like the look on the doctor's face when he asked, "You never saw the pills? The medication? You lived here quite a while before you went off to college, didn't you?"

The young man turned to the doctor. He had been directing his words out toward the bay, but now he confronted the doctor's presumptuous red little face. "I don't think you can understand the kind of relationship we had. We never said all that much to each other. I never knew he was sick." And then, pointedly, "Except of course he drank too much."

The doctor looked away from the young man, looked out to the bay and said, "He wasn't that far gone the day he died. He could have saved himself. He was sitting right here where I'm sitting, and the pills were just about twenty feet away inside the living room. The pills were on the table. All he had to do was to get up—which I believe he could have done—and get those pills."

Inside his head, the young man finished the doctor's supposition—if someone had cared enough to stay here and take care of him, then that someone would have administered the pills. Stewart would still be alive today.

But the doctor no longer troubled or irritated the young man. He looked out over the opiate beauty of the sea, and he saw with Stewart's gray and unwavering watery eyes. He knew that when the pains struck they were distant pains—attacking a body that was no longer a part of the real life of the man. He had finally entered that realm he had been longing for. Whatever part of his brain reminded him of the pills also knew that they would be a meaningless barrier against his slide to the sea. And since so much of his existence had already been washed away, it seemed that a bottle of pills was no more than a pathetic sandbag—the use of which was to stem the inevitable.

He just sat there and remained still because he was already in possession of the drug he needed.

"You are becoming hollowed into a husk," he had said to the young man all those years ago. And it may have been the last time he had taken a close look at another human being—his coconspirator in the attempted looting of beauty.

The doctor interrupted with a cracked voice (he needed a drink), "So. What are your plans? Gonna buy a house out here?"

"Not right now. I guess I'll just go back to Boston."

"Law school," the doctor said, standing. "Good money in law—that's for sure."

"Yes. There is. Maybe it won't be such a bad life."

It was a curious thing to say, but for the most part, the doctor's mind was no longer on the subject. "I wonder if there's a little scotch in that house." And he walked toward the living room. Over his shoulder he said, "If things don't work out in Boston, you can always come back out here. You won't be the first to change your mind and come back out to where you belong."

Ocean Boy

When the highly acclaimed marine biologist thought back to his seventeenth spring—which was often—he would focus his memory on one particular night. Through a membranous lens confluent with eroticism and despair, he would examine this particle of time he had designated as the night of the witness. He would excite himself—provoke the green culture of his imagination that had grown positively hairy with life through all the years of embellishment. He would perform a ribald tease on the stage of memory and then exit through wings of depression.

The finale was always the same. A sardonic flip to the last page of this comic-strip installment and the legend of the series gaudily scrawled across a consciousness poised to return from break—reapply to vocation. The colorful letters formed this title: *The Night the Land Creatures* (one in particular) *Discovered Who William Bohan Actually Was!*

Spring of 1968—a period of transition that resulted in a disoriented state of being rivaled only by the misadventurous escape from the lagoon of pulp.

He was poor, yet he was on his way to one of the great institutions of learning in the world—Massachusetts Institute of Technology. He had been an unknown wallflower all of his life, and then in June of his seventeenth year, he had landed in the pages of the *Cape Cod Times* because he had won a scholarship.

Everyone in his tiny hometown of Craigville knew what was happening to him, and they gawked at his appearance in supermarkets and in minimalls. Some people were mean to him. Billy Bohan could be walking down Main Street in his dreamy way and have his watery brains pierced by comments from teenagers on the corner. They would say things like, "Asshole's into ocean gigs when everyone knows space is where it's at." And sometimes the kids' limited vocabulary was laced with implications of queerness simply because Billy was not known to indulge in social intercourse. Which was because he had never found the company of human beings very interesting.

In this his last spring and summer of small-town life, he could still find solitude in a place he had always thought of as the secret cove. A parcel of beach on the glacial slide that was Cape Cod. An outdoor laboratory that was actually the birthplace of his subsequently acclaimed talents.

The tranquility he had always found at the cove was equaled by the buffer-state mentality of his home. After the age of seven, he had been raised solely by a free-thinking father, a product of the rambunctious sixties. A painter who did portraits of tourists in summer for the money and painted his own less commercial visions during the rest of the year.

After Billy's mother died of heart failure at the age of twenty-seven, he had for company over the next ten years one cool and unflappable Dad. Nothing Billy ever said to this man invited reprimands. For instance, this (at age thirteen), "I think sharks smile like women, Dad. Like Jenny's smiling at you right now." And he gestured toward the young model who sat naked while William Bohan Senior worked on her portrait. "But have you ever noticed how porpoises smile like effeminate men? They're bisexual, you know. Me, I'd rather have sex with a porpoise than a shark."

And his long-haired father replied with a cackled answer spoken in the idiom of the era, "Well, Billy boy. Different strokes for different folks." And turned his fully seductive attention back to the model, who waited impatiently for Billy to leave.

The secret cove was located on the shores of Nantucket Sound, nestled into Squaw Island, which bordered Hyannis Port. A two-mile bike ride from where he lived—the shoreline curved inward on this part of the beach—afforded a concave hideaway within a shroud of trees and shrubs.

In later years, he would ruminate on the poetry of his find because the discovery happened directly after his mother's death. That he had actually curled up inside a penetrable dent beneath the green and swirling pubic hairs of nature became a delightful and morbidly erotic memory. He would see himself in the sand at seven, his legs open wide, lying in wait for the rush of ocean that would fuck-pound the shore and release into the cove its foamy cum to lap the naked babe—a plethora of kisses upon his spongy penis.

The breakwater was located near the cove, and at low tide he would crouch upon certain rocks that teemed with life during various times of the year. He would stare at barnacle shells nearly obsessively after it became known to him that there were actually animals inside. He would crouch with the palm of his hand over rockweed and run his fingers through algae. He would take mussels back to the cove, feeling like a murderer, and he would cut open the shells to probe the flesh inside.

By the time he was twelve, his father allowed him to sleep overnight at the cove on occasional summer nights. He would arrive at low tide to inspect the life and death the retreating waters had left behind. And then after spending hours by fading sunlight and flashlight examining his catch, he would swim naked in the dark. For sensual pleasure (in place of sport) and to allow the ocean to inspect his body in, no doubt, the same curious way he so shamelessly gawked at the life of the ocean.

He felt covered with eyes as he swam, and one night as he traveled low to the ocean floor, the feel of seaweed produced in him the oddest sensation he had ever known. He surfaced in water where he could stand and gripped his erection. Then dove under again, weaving in and out of the silky grass until he sent scurrying into the ocean the first seeds of his body's new life. Afterward he slept in the peace of the cove, dreaming of fantastic impregnations.

He grew to be tall and thin—the body of a barracuda. Although his mother and father were blond, Billy had black hair, which he wore long because he forgot to cut it (without regard to the fact that long hair on boys was fashionable). Mom and Dad were both brown-eyed. Billy was green. He was small-boned, which did not match the physiques of his parents. His Dad laughingly wondered where the nose could have come from. A thin and prominent hawklike nose which adolescents made fun of but which—years later in the cities—adult women and gays would find sexy. He was always tanned, of course, with his brilliant white and shy smile a tease because the distant green eyes were of a distraction that precluded intimacy. He thought of his eyes as too prominently bulged, and he attributed this to all the time spent underwater. He never wore goggles. It was important that the sea life saw him as he actually was—without artifice.

For seventeen years—until his last months on the Cape—he had never sought out friendship. He fantasized of having a best friend and was convinced that there was no live version of this boy to be found among his peers. He would not even think of asking a Cape boy to engage in the activities that he and the dream boy found so pleasurable. And there was one major plus in keeping his friendship fantastic—changeability. One day he wanted his best friend to be blond and muscular, and the next day he would make him thin and dark-haired—a twin. Hair on the chest was nice whenever he felt vulnerable and in need of protection. Other times a smooth chest like his own could act as an antidote to the threatening aspects of sex.

The boy would come to the cove at night after Billy had collected and examined specimens. Naked, they would swim rather acrobatically underwater. Billy would plunge beneath his friend—whose name changed constantly—and then approach him from the back, glide across the length of the boy's body—the only contact that of his penis in a seconds-only slide against moss inside the crack of ass. And while Billy circled for another pass, the boy would roll over and swim on his back, and when Billy crossed above, he would clutch both penises in his two hands and they would swim like that until their sperm was released into the sea. A milky spray of spermatozoa that intermingled and then danced like sea urchins all around the boys.

Everything was water, and eyes were the proof that everything was related to everything. He could look into the eyes of a squid and sense familiarity. The incredibly ugly angler fish appeared as a disembodied human head with eyes more spookily familiar than any in the ocean. As horrible looking as the angler was, how could any human look into its eyes and not feel touched by primitive remembrance?

It was easy to make the connections in life outside the ocean too, of course, but sea creatures lived within the source of the soul. The soul was water—a bottomless pool inside even the tiniest creature. And the history of all existence floated in every-one's pool. If you remained quiet for an extended period of time—as he did floating on top of the water—you could feel ancient senses stirring (and it got so he could feel this lying in the sand also). You could just know that the life of the planet was down there bubbling in the pool, although very little in the way of hard news ever surfaced to consciousness. Probably because of blocks imposed by human teachings.

In the spring of 1968, the dream boy perished by lack of imagination. Billy found himself going to Craigville Beach, a popular hangout for kids his age. It was a mating beach really, where the two sexes sought each other out. It was a beach he had not visited since discovering the cove ten years before. And it was a beach—since he suffered no confusion concerning the focus of his desire—where he did not belong. Still, he could lie there and look—and go slightly berserk with horniness.

Nothing in his scientific life had prepared him for what quick-ly mushroomed into a fixation on all things male. He would look at the boys on the beach with a knot in his throat, a feeling of suffocation, because he could not have them. His great tri-umph—acceptance at MIT—was overwhelmed by considerations of his aloneness in human affairs. How could he have missed the foresight that there was, after all, something in humanity he could use?

Use? If they gave him half a chance, he would devour it.

He was rational enough to know that he still did not really want any involvement with anyone. He could be perfectly happy with the life at his cove and without the social amenities of small-town life if he could just have maybe thirty minutes a day "doing it" with a real live boy.

The other kids had no idea—as he passed among them in school or on the street—that though his attitude seemed to be as socially indifferent as ever, a part of him had virtually metamorphosed.

How could he approach other boys for the one thing he wanted when he wanted nothing else? He was so far removed from their interests that one afternoon, exiting the school in a crowd of students, he had impulsively turned to a boy walking next to him and asked, "How come the flags are half-mast?"

The kid looked at him with eyes that dangled the word "jerk" in the air. "Bobby Kennedy," he said tersely.

"Yeah? So? Oh. You mean he died?"

The boy stopped and addressed the students flowing around him. "Do you believe this nerd is asking me if Bobby Kennedy died?"

He told his father about this when he arrived home, and his father—for the first time he could recall—looked at him with a bit of trepidation. "Well, it's the reason why I've been down lately, Billy. I mean, he wasn't just a famous politician running for president. He lived in the next town over. You even met him once."

No. Conversation with these beings he needed was out of the question. And his days of going to Craigville Beach were coming to an end because of the MIT announcement in the paper—complete with high school yearbook photo. He had probably been at least somewhat obvious in his aloneness on the beach (sneaking furtive glances with peripheral vision), but now, with media notoriety, some of the kids had begun to stare at him.

And so, on a humid day during the second week of June, he pedaled his bike out to this fertile crescent of beach where stalks and fruits were dangled provocatively so that the human race might continue. But as he locked his bike at the rack in the parking lot that skirted the beach, he was damaged in spirit by a premonition of premature decrepitude. He was a poacher on this beach. He was there only to mentally confiscate the breeder's seed. How awful that he should be turning into a Peeping Tom when he himself possessed the beauty of adolescence and should therefore be among the young who were peeped.

Depressed and tense, he decided to leave but first went to the cooler near the rest rooms for a swallow of water. Wishing for nothing less than invisibility among these aliens, he dipped for a quick drink and then enraged himself by guzzling down the wrong pipe. He straightened up coughing, doubled over hacking and spitting, and through it all suffered hot flashes of embarrassment.

And then there was a hand on his back helping to slap up water and a voice in his ear that said, "Hey! You're Bohan! MIT!"

He was finally able to gain control of himself and as he straightened and turned, the boy said, "The only Cape man to make MIT! My father went there. Congratulations."

A confluence of impressions that scored a direct hit on his wounded libido. The boy's words had been perfectly enunciated, Hyannis Port as opposed to the muted, dreary voices of Craigville. There was the mention of a father at MIT delivered with the cheer of money to spare (and so again—Hyannis Port). The vocal range was high and the appearance was on the outlandish side, which only the ego of the rich can bring off with confidence. Into this coop of the redneck had flown a fair blond swan. A slender boy of medium height and fine features dressed in two towels—one wet and suggestive around the hips, the other wrapped on top of his head—blond waves streaked down over the ears. What a glut of self-assuredness! Only girls wrapped their hair in towels—he must have security guards with machine guns watching from a nearby limo. His eyes were a large blue, filled with curiosity. But the detail on this bronzed and brown-nippled body that was most responsible for the pouchful of tickles inside Billy's cutoffs was the hips. Billy read an invitation written by Mother Nature on the width of these hips. There was the tapering of chest and stomach to delicate waist and then this insouciant voluptuous curvature of hips—genes drunk on androgyny! And the biologist in Billy (that part of him which could stay cool inside heat) informed him that here on this beach, at last, stood one of his own. There could be no other purpose to these hips than to beckon the mate who sought the masculine inside the sway of the effeminate. The towels for a wardrobe came natural—to distinguish the breed and to indicate the grace with which he would be fully revealed. Billy, staring open-mouthed at the boy, saw one hand raised exotically to free the flowing blond hair while the other hand simply flicked away the bottom towel with easy abandon. There could be no doubt that the actual vision lay in the immediate future.

A moment of disorientation shook Billy from his rapture. A hand thrust out to shake his own. "I'm John Roberts." And a grip too firm—a breach of image. But then he was a boy raised to socialize, was he not? And protective mannerisms at the advent of their destiny would not be so unusual either. "I'm off to Harvard in September. You must be on top of the world. I know I am." All of this said in a terribly boyish rush of great seriousness so unlike the students at Billy's school.

Billy said, "Yes. Me too. It feels great." And he heard himself in an unusually high-gear tone of voice, as though both had been trained to recognize each other through a code designed in decibels.

John Roberts could relax now, and he simultaneously shifted weight onto one foot while a hand so delicate it might have been recently unwebbed perched on a tilted hip. "I'll bet my father would enjoy meeting you. He was engineering at MIT. Drops a ton of money on the place every year. You're oceanography, right?"

"Yes."

"Are you doing anything tonight? Can you come over? It would have to be after dinner. My mother has this thing about short notice. But if you're free around eight, I know my dad would really love to meet you."

"I'd very much like to meet your dad." Said in cheerful obei-
sance to any formality that was tranquil balm to John's hidden
agenda.

"The address is 55 Irving. Expect trouble getting through. The
Bobby thing has completely upset our social lives. I think those
damn Kennedys expect a full-scale attack on the compound any
time now. But I'll leave your name with security at the corner of
Scudder and Irving. Just make sure you have I.D."

"I'll remember. Sure, okay."

"You can talk to my dad for a while and then you and I can
take a walk. Fill me in on oceanography. All I know about the
ocean relates to sailing. By the way. Is it William or Bill?"

"Bill."

And another vigorous shake of hands, but now John Roberts
was smiling. "Look forward to seeing you, Bill. See you later."

But as the boy turned to walk away, the smile lingered for just
a split second on Billy's face, as though reluctant to go without
some subliminal message. The smile softened with regret, and
then just as he began to step away, one hand went up to rescue a
slipping towel. A readjustment and consequent shiver of cheeks
beneath the towel. A quick look back at Billy—this time a smile
turned mischievous.

His father had gone out with his latest conquest—another model—for the evening and so Billy did not have to explain why he
left the house in his "dress-up clothes" on such a hot and sticky
night. Confused as to what to wear for passage through portals of
the wealthy, he had selected the clothes he had worn for testing
and interviews at MIT in Cambridge.

Wearing a long-sleeved white shirt, corduroys, and thick,
heavy black shoes, he was miserably uncomfortable riding his
bike the two-mile distance to Hyannis Port. The last part of the
journey on Scudder Avenue was a quarter of a mile uphill, and
his body was bathed in sweat and his nerves in a rare state of
anxiety as he wondered how to act with a family so foreign to his
background. And much more important, how could he gracefully

and quickly remove John and himself to their summer abode, the cove on Squaw Island?

But it turned out that he was only expected to remain in the large, sprawling white house for fifteen minutes. This was a perfunctory visit, as John's father was brought into the hall where he waited. It was as though anyone touched by notoriety was expected to check in with Mr. Roberts for quick inspection. Billy felt like a village subject congratulated by royalty as, with John Jr. by his side, he stood in front of a tall, barrel-chested man dressed in Bermuda shorts and a sports shirt. He had distinguished-looking gray hair and he smelled of gin. The entire time they stood in the hallway, Billy could not take his eyes off eyebrows that slithered unbroken like a fat caterpillar across a blown-out red face.

He alluded to MIT just once. "Ah! Here he is! The only guy out here who could make the grade. Welcome to the club, Bill!"

Billy felt ridiculous standing there sweating in his heavy clothes while John Jr., long, silky blond hair parted in the middle, stood next to him wearing adorable snug-fitting white shorts and white T-shirt (HYANNIS PORT CLUB etched in blue across his heart).

Mr. Roberts clamped a hand on Billy's shoulder. "Wanna drink, Bill? Come out on the terrace and join us for a while? We're celebrating the removal of that punk down the street from the big race."

Billy nodded and tried a low register of voice to compete a bit with Mr. Robert's domineering growl. "Yes. The Teddy Kennedy murder. Changes the complexion of the race."

The caterpillar buckled on the big red face and John Jr. said, "He's oceanography, Dad. Not politics. Let's go, Bill." And he turned him toward the door, saying to his father, "I'm about to get some quick oceanographic instruction."

Outside on Irving Avenue, Billy took note of the crowds of people extending all the way down to the harbor, three blocks away. In his nervousness on his way to the Roberts' house, he had ignored this bizarre scene. He had not even paused to think about what was going on when he had had to show I.D. to a security man. For the second time that week, he became haunted by an awareness of his ignorance. The boy walking next to him had to think he was a freak. But then his eyes dipped down to the white tennis shoes walking by his side and took in with a glance the brown legs populated with blond fuzz, and he was lost in a reverie of what John Roberts would look like naked.

"If we cut down Dale Avenue to Barrier Beach, we should be able to lose these crowds," John said, and he seemed just as sociable as he had been when they met that afternoon. So they turned off Irving and onto Dale, stopping once at a driveway that led to the Kennedy compound to show guards their I.D., John explaining that Billy was a guest of his family.

They rounded a curve of Dale that overlooked Nantucket Sound and walked down a steep hill that led to Squaw Island Road and Barrier Beach. Sounding tactful while looking Billy up and down, John said, "I'm sorry. I should have loaned you shorts for the beach. It really is hot out tonight."

"That's okay. I know a good place to swim where you don't need shorts or suits." He grinned because even as he said it this prospect made him happy.

And John grinned right back. "We all have our skinny-dipping spots. Oh, by the way, while you waited for Dad to get away from his guests I put your bike in the garage. Now tell me. How did you get interested in oceanography?"

"I think it started with sand crabs. When I was a kid, I was really fascinated with sand crabs."

John looked at him expressionlessly and nodded. "Uh-huh. That's interesting."

"What are you gonna take up at Harvard?"

"Well, I'm going to be a lawyer."

"What made you want to be a lawyer?"

And the grin came back to spread across his face. "Money! Money got me interested in law. Ah, shit! Just look at that! Those dumb bastards are guarding the entrance to the island too."

He meant a couple of security guards who had set up a road-block at the entrance to Squaw Island. But Billy was titillated by the boy's outburst. It had been so petulant. It reminded him of the tantrums his father's models threw so often when they accused him of going out with other models. The sound of John's voice had been peevish and girlish, and again renewed the sense of possibilities for the evening (which had been dimmed by the dreary meeting with Mr. Roberts).

The suggested walk to Barrier Beach had been perfect because it led to the cove. And the sandy road they walked upon at the moment ran between the beach on the east side and the wetlands on the west—in full view of security; they would have to check with them before they could use the beach that wrapped around the island.

They stopped on the road, John still fuming. "I forgot those damn Kennedys have property on Squaw Island too." But then he brightened. "I know what we'll do. The Crowleys have the first house on the beach side. I'll tell the agents we're on our way to the Crowleys and if they want they can call them. Then we'll stop off at the Crowleys, I'll borrow a bottle of wine, and we'll go find this place of yours."

Twenty minutes later, they walked in the dark on the part of the beach that was down from the Crowley place. John held a bottle of wine in one hand, two glasses in the other. Billy had a flashlight in his hand, given to him by the Crowleys, though he did not need or use it. He felt melancholy over the fact that they had been permitted onto a beach that he had, so many years ago, taken for his own. He had wanted John to have a sense of the conspirator as they made their way to the cove. It was Billy's beach, and he had chaffed under the invitation of fake owners to enter his own habitat. And he had wanted John to have the erotic sense of the outlaw when they were naked, just as he had always had. Nothing could make you feel more wild and free than the possibility that you might be discovered in the act of that freedom and made to pay in some way. A forbidden mood—so essential to his sexual longing—seemed to have dissipated.

"How much farther?" John asked after a while. He had been whistling, happy ever since the Crowleys had laid the wine in his hand.

"Just a ways up there where the beach curves." A horn moon had been revealed as clouds drifted off, and Billy knew he had to shake off his moodiness as he looked at John walking slightly ahead of him. But the boy seemed like an intruder carrying the wine and glasses, as though he were about to view an art exhibition.

"You know," John sang out, "I think I've probably taken my kayak in around these parts."

The tide was on its way in as they reached the indentation of the shoreline. They walked into the cove and sat down next to each other where the sand was dry, backs to a low wall of shrubs. A sticky breeze rustled the leaves of the trees beyond the shrubs, and the sliver of moon provided a faint night-light. Billy thought of the smile on John's face as he had hitched up his towel that afternoon. It had to have been a flirtatious smile, hadn't it? And he thought of the self-assurance his father had with the models he painted. How, if his father was attracted to a woman, she ended up in his bed. And if his father had been in his shoes this afternoon and had found himself attracted to John, the game would have been over just as soon as John had flashed that provocative smile. Billy's father would have taken John off someplace without hesitation.

Because his father knew people and would have known enough to pounce immediately. His father listened to people and he watched them and knew their habits.

Whereas Billy had never even been interested in what people were like.

Back home earlier, getting dressed to go to the Roberts' house, he had had the most difficult time trying to remember the school John had been accepted by. He could think of round ass beneath a wet, clinging towel and wonderful blue eyes and erect brown nipples, but very little of what the boy had said. He had thought that signals had gone out between them by means of a sexual sonar. Decisions had been made without unnecessary communication.

He had thought of John the way he thought of himself—as a creature who still belonged to the ocean. He had even imagined the smile as the mating call of a mermaid.

If they had only gone off together as soon as they had met, there would have been no communication needed. They could have come here to the cove and hidden in the spaces between the shrubs. There would not have been these social amenities of the family and visit with the Crowleys that drummed into Billy the uselessness of what he was outside the confines of his inner oceanic life. He would not be staring down into the sand now, mute with the despair of believing he would never be equipped to be with anyone.

John said, "Do you have a girl?"

And Billy realized that the boy was nervous—the tone of voice shaky. He poured wine and handed a glass to Billy. Then he poured himself a glass, drank it down, and poured another. Sirens sounded over in Hyannis Port and Billy wondered if yet another human being he knew nothing about had been murdered.

"No. I don't have a girl." Said deliberately because he felt ignited by John's uneasiness. He put the glass in the sand.

"You're like me. No commitments until after college."

"I'm going for a swim. I've been in these stupid hot clothes long enough." He stood and stripped, and as he walked out to the water he heard John say, "No lights on anywhere. I suppose it's all right."

But after walking out to meet the tide, he swam just a short distance before anger had him turning back. A sense of all his father had gotten away with sexually. The feeling that somehow he had been cheated.

He had rushed out into the water and come back in again so quickly that John—naked now—was just tentatively inching in up to his knees. He was not at home with the ocean, and he reached both hands down to splash just the way old people do when they have gone as far as their courage will take them.

Billy picked a spot on the shore where he could lie on his back and have the tide's foam ooze around his body. He lay there propped on his elbows watching John. He looked so vulnerable naked and bent over. At the mercy of the sea. So light and small and easily taken. "If he were out in the water far enough," Billy thought, "I would swim up from behind and bite his ass."

He turned and started to walk back to shore, and Billy looked at the shriveled penis that could have been a beach plum in the tangle of his wet blond bush. His own penis did not shrink in the ocean; most of the time it was erect, and though that was not the case now, it still rested plump on his sagging balls.

He tried not to see, but John was just too beautiful emerging from the water. The boy had the ocean for a cape upon his back and the gold of his hair gave to him the aura of a child bewitched by the moon. And the startling white flesh between the bands of brown on his body was enough to make Billy finally turn his head away.

John lay down in the sand, a little farther apart from Billy than when they had sat together in the cove. The sound of his voice came as unnatural while they lay in the water. "I don't think I've ever met anyone with as little to say as you. I suppose you're very preoccupied with your studies or else you never would have made it to MIT."

"Ocean's pretty much all I ever knew." And he stared straight ahead. What would it be like out in the world? Would everyone be immune to his feelings?

"What do you do for fun?"

"This is it. Pretty much what I'm doing right now." A piece of kelp floated up around his feet, and he reached for it and placed it over his penis. He resented John now, and he looked over at him and said, "Most valuable food in the world."

With a nervous laugh, John said, "Slimiest food in the world."

Seaweed was beginning to float in all around them now, and Billy took a clump of the stuff and tossed it over to John who surprised him by passively allowing the plant to land on his thigh. Watching the boy reclining back on his arms and staring at the kelp, Billy's erection lifted his own plant and he giggled. He took strands of the kelp and tied it around his cock—looking at John while he worked. The boy looked fascinated and Billy moved quickly to his side, slid the kelp to John's rising cock and passed the kelp over slowly, watching the boy stiffen. He said, "Feels good, huh?"—filled with hope—loving the fact that John had been lured by both sea and boy.

The smack on the back of his head made his ears ring, and then he was looking up at John who stood above him, kelp-free but hard. "I was afraid of this. I knew there was something wrong with you when I introduced myself this afternoon. But I decided to give you the benefit of the doubt."

"What?" He didn't care what John said if he would just stand there and let Billy look. The first man he had ever seen. Huge. The bush of hair, dry now and swirling, maddening to look at.

"You know what I'm talking about. You bastard! You really thought I was like you!"

Somehow he had to keep him there, but all he could think of to say was, "Well, don't knock it till you've tried it. You can't have that much against it with a hard-on like that."

But John turned and then he was walking up the beach, stopping halfway to where his clothes lay and looking back said, "You ever see me around this summer don't even think of coming up to me. I'm gonna put the word out on you—queer."

Billy lay back in the sand and closed his eyes. To keep the vision. To at least not let the boy take the vision away with him. He rearranged it all the way he wanted it—saw John lying next to him with legs apart. Watched seaweed swimming up between his legs. The pull of tide had made a hole beneath his ass and he watched the plant float to the estuary around his anus. He watched himself sitting on John's thighs, tying their cocks together with seaweed. And then it was all around them—carried in by small waves, moving over their bodies, retreating back into the ocean, surging around them again. The moon expanded and became full to illuminate and make sparkle the sea drops all over the boy's body. Magically, there were drops on his nipples, and he licked them away and then glued his mouth to his willing partner. Sucked the juices from his mouth, tasting the coat of wine across his tongue. Cupped with one hand some seawater, disengaged from John's mouth, and drank without swallowing. He slid down now as the tide rose and lapped them with ocean and foam and kelp, and he untied the two bursting cocks and took the boy into his mouth. He let the seawater swirl around John's cock and then spit it out and brought his mouth to his ear to whisper. To tell him that at age twelve he had made the discovery that sperm tasted like the ocean. Had experimented with himself and now he had John. He would drink it out of him but save enough to bring to his lips. Because it meant so much to him that he should know. Know that it was this that he wanted from him. The ocean that was inside him.

He opened his eyes to look at his stomach—the pool of juice spreading and dripping over his sides. A scoop to his mouth and another association besides the seawater—the taste of clams.

He craned his head around to see John, fully dressed, running along the beach to Hyannis Port. He really would tell some of the other boys. For the rest of the summer, he would have to be careful when he came here. Or maybe it was over and he should not ever come again.

John was way down the beach now, scrambling to the top of breakers—rocks cold and remote as the moon's. And then he was leaping from the breakers—his gold head a firefly suspended in the night for just a moment before disappearing forever from Billy's view.

While William Bohan—ascending star in the constellation of the water-logged sciences—walked out into the ocean beneath the horn moon sky. He vigorously dove into the water and swam for half of a lifetime. His star never ceased to climb even as he navigated through decades of sterility.

Today he has many versions of the night he was discovered by the land creature. But since the two have been married for so long—making love through waves of decades—he has days when he scientifically ruminates about the central imperfection of the relationship. He constructs a rather lovely drama around the imperfection—the fact that there never actually was a physical union. He is creative enough to live within the marriage one day and then to awaken the next day within the wonder of unrequited love. But a tale of unrequited love like no other.

John Roberts had initially been both attracted and aroused when he had met Billy Bohan. But it was the half-formed self that he had discovered in Billy during their rendezvous that had put John off. Bad timing. He had witnessed Billy during his crawl from ocean to land, while the boy had struggled on his belly across the dry terrain of social graces. The boy was simply late for his appointment with evolution. And John Roberts, fairly steeped within the aggravations of the civilization, had been appalled by this primitive whose only accomplishment thus far had been his single-minded rise to the top of the food chain.

Bohan felt sure that in the decades since their encounter, John, possibly during tedious times of passage, had been aroused by the memory of the transitional creature that was Billy. It was just so unfortunate that they had missed each other by maybe only a thousand years or so.

The Shih Tzu Master's Thermos

Rembrandt would have loved using the heavy press of paint to convey the long story in the shifting moods of his craggy, thick-boned face. A tall face, broad, with a large nose and flaring nostrils and blue eyes that were severe, or demented, but most often shone and danced the way those long, gangling legs once sparked the boards of Broadway. Pouches like small eggs beneath the eyes, two meandering hairy caterpillars above. A thick wide mouth hard as the shell of an oyster with pearls of white tiny teeth inside. He either spoke with the excitable whisper of a gossipy debutante or the roar of a disgruntled sea captain intolerant of all the mutinies that invade a dreamer's life. Everything was important—necessary. He could not phone a pizza parlor without sounding desperate.

I think he was somewhere around seventy when I knew him back in the eighties, and he loved to drink. Maintained a lifelong flirtation with cocaine too. But oh, man, the drinking! Out in Provincetown where life is lived by so many of the locals on the broad rim of a chowder-bowl-sized shot glass. Christian could drink all day and all night on binges—vodka reacting on his system like amphetamines.

He was born in Provincetown, spent some time in New York as a Broadway chorus boy, and then returned home for good in the forties to ply the trade of a bartender (equivalent to entering a religious order in Provincetown). In the old days, he numbered among his friends Tennessee Williams and Marlon Brando who summered in Provincetown. He even shared a cottage with Brando, and it must have been a mind-boggling time in which to live. It was the years after World War II, and the struggle for coexistence in that part of the world meant keeping the peace among poets and redneck fishermen. Antiquated winds of Catholic ethos still remained to ruffle the wigs of summer queens from New York and Boston. Christian told me he had a ball.

When I lived in Provincetown, I would go over to the two-floor house he rented at the end of a sandy alley in the center of town. He was the proud "father" of twenty-two mangy Shih Tzu dogs, and as he opened the door to greet me, these swarming piranha would attack en masse, looking as though the carnivorous rug of the floor was rolling itself up to break through walls just to get at my feet.

Watching him walk the dogs was a special treat. He used to walk down the street with all twenty-two branches of leashes attached to one lead. Arriving at a small park he stopped near bushes, waiting for the dogs to obey nature's call. They all tried to pull him this way and that, but he would stand his ground, although swaying to and fro—a drunken maestro conducting a thoroughly rebellious orchestra. He cajoled—loudly exhorted sections to squeeze out their notes—gesturing to one side and then the other, all the while smiling blissfully, lost in the beauty of chaotic creation. And when one of the orchestra sounded a harmonious note at last, he would sweep one free arm in the air and shout, "Bravo! Bravo!"

I think now of his hair—a tangled explosion of exotic messages from the screaming brains beneath—down almost to his shoulders in wild grays tinged with brown. He had the hair of a Portuguese sea captain who navigates hatless and wears the turbulence of nor'easter winds upon his head. Of a chemist electrified by the consumption of his own bizarre experiments. Then, too, you could place Christian's scalp on the floor and behold the twenty-third Shih Tzu.

I can explain my hesitation in describing Christian's wardrobe by saying that the interior of his rented house resembled a ridiculously overstocked warehouse. All living creatures inside the house were an imposition on space. He had not thrown out a single article of clothing in over four decades, and closet doors and trunks remained open twenty-four hours a day to accommodate his daily demand for variety in dress. To take a fling at Christian's fashions would be to write a catalog book. For instance, hats. Somewhere around forty years ago he worked in a hat shop, and when the owner died, Christian inherited all the hats that were scattered everywhere around the house, including the kitchen and inside the ancient auto too. He had the hats stuffed in the trunk of the car and packed into the backseat from floor to ceiling. Riding up front with him, an unexpected press of the brakes would prompt an avalanche of hats all over driver and guest in the same way that an arm casually flung over the back of a sofa in the living room caused hats to tumble like heads off the block of an automated guillotine. Christian just adored hats.

It was inexplicable to me how this ex-student of dance seemed to hold up Jerry Lewis as a role model of grace. Drunk or sober, he was a klutz. He attempted the role of grand host, but he was dangerous to be around, as objects fell wherever he walked. I learned early never to stand near him holding a drink in my hand. And the one time I stayed as an overnight guest was outrageous enough so that I never repeated my mistake.

I had had a flu all day but still kept a promise to stop by his house for a drink. Feeling awful, I let him talk me into staying for stew, which according to Christian was "a marvelous cure-all for all that ails you." I ate the stuff even though I knew his stew to be a general house cleaning of all foods on the brink of mold thrown into a pot and left to simmer all day. With an optimism born of drinking his screwdrivers (glasses showing only the palest shade of orange), I figured that among all the ingredients in the pot there had to be at least one that could act as an antidote to influenza. But the stew tasted worse than usual that night, and when I asked what the green things floating in the bowl were, he answered that they were "my vodka limes. They've become a trifle soft and so I thought they might add a dash of vitamin C to the potpourri. I was concerned with the rasp of your voice on the phone, darling." Oh. And that acrid smell? "Why valerian to relax the patient."

Since our table was dominated, as always, by a half-gallon jug of Gordon's vodka, dinner lasted until close to midnight, by which time I was burning with fever. I got up from the table to leave, but he grabbed my arm, saucer eyes shot through with alarm. "I cannot allow you to leave my house in this condition, darling. My Gawd! Ptomaine could strike at any second! I'll get you one of my robes right after I finish my drink and put you up on the sofa. What color robe would you prefer? What style? My collection is on the second floor. We'll have a fitting."

I was too far gone to shop the second-floor emporium so I let him go up alone, murmuring as he went up the stairs about results from a study he had read "that proves how marvelously effective bright colors can be to the patient in his struggle with disease."

As my head lay sleeping on the table, he took close to an hour to select a robe of delirious psychedelic colors. I was very tense as he undressed me in the kitchen because he did so with a cigarette in his mouth, coming awfully close to naked parts and frequently losing his balance while he unbuttoned, unzipped, pulled, and at one point dropped ashes on the pouch of my briefs.

Once dressed we fought our way through the booby-trapped living room full of cascading hats and open trunks that had great black capes slithering out like vampires from their caskets, and there were ballroom dresses and loud zoot suits hanging out of the trunks and flocks of scarves and what appeared to be striped prison wear. We had to stumble through nests of belts all over the floor, and my soft, slippered feet had to be wary of cutting but interestingly designed pornographic weather vanes and name-brand electric liquor signs taken from ancient saloons.

He cleared the sofa of western hats, mouseketeer ears, bonnets, fedoras, and seafaring caps. Smothering me in blankets, he was almost endearingly protective, except for the fact that he would not accommodate my wish to have the police scanner turned off. It was hooked up there in the living room, not far from my aching head, and I knew he kept it going all night long. His bedroom was just off the living room, and there was no space for a table on which to place the scanner because he used that room to house his collection of ships' anchors. He kept the door open, explaining that while he slept all mention of police encounters with his many relatives and lifelong acquaintances climbed into his brain to be recalled in the morning. He pointed out, as he fluffed up pillows, that it was always wise to be apprised of criminal activity among the people in your circle. "You see, luv, such information is currency in forestalling attacks on one's reputation. It pays for silence in advance."

In spite of the bored monotone of Provincetown cops speaking through the static of the speakers, I was sick enough to fall asleep quickly. But sometime in the middle of the night, I was awakened by a burning pain. Not inside my chest but on top of my chest. In a panic, my hand went to my chest only to wallow in molten goo. My eyes flew open to find Christian bent over me with a plate in his hand, a horrified expression on the face inches from my own. "Ohhh, Gawd, luv! Don't be alarmed! There is a remarkably tasty, simmering grilled cheese attached to your bosom. I thought you might be hungry. But I must do something with my collection of crutches, luv. You see, that's how I tripped. Crutches sticking out from under the sofa. Are you hurt, luv? Come now, sit up. The sandwich is still good. I'll just scrape it off your chest. I'm sure the heat was beneficial. But please, luv, eat it before it gets cold. I went to a lot of trouble. And by the time you're through, the stew should be ready. I added the limes from our drinks tonight. Preserved by the vodka to ensure sterilization. Ascorbic acid, luv. You'll be cured by morning. Ohhhh, Gawd! I think we should call the doctor! Complications have set in! There appear to be third-degree burns on your chest, luv!"

*   *   *

My first memory of him—in a bar in 1981—is dim because I was drunk. But before I lost it completely that night, I can still see this enormous face peering into my own from the neighboring bar stool. Great nostrils of a stallion breathing fire, crazed blue eyes moving like Mexican jumping beans. A broad mouth full of uncommonly small baby teeth. He was smiling approval at me, and his breath was unbelievable. The unmistakable stink of squid stew mixed with the fumes of a day's drinking. "Ahhhh"— exhaling the rot of squid into my face—"you do love your Jack Daniels, I can see. My father drank entire vats of Jack Daniels every day of his life and lived to be ninety-five. Allow me to buy you a drink and so add years to your longevity, my young friend. Bartender! A triple Jack Daniels for my newfound soul mate! Compensation for paradise lost!"

It was one of his cocaine nights, but he never behaved noticeably drugged on these rare occasions. In fact, he was pretty much the same on or off alcohol too. It was completely in character for him when, before the drink even reached my hand, he had me standing before his bar stool, hands in the air. And then he reached inside my coat to stuff his fingers into my armpits, withdrew and proclaimed to the rest of the people at the bar, "I knew it! Drenched with sweat! His glands are healthy! And he owes it all to Mr. Jack Daniels!"

He knew all the year-round locals, and they all certainly knew Christian. In spite of his late nights, he got up at five every morning and worked as an administrator in a home for the elderly. He once rounded up a dozen or so of the residents one day around noon, having diagnosed the chosen ones as in need of a "spiritual life," and brought them down to the Commercial Street bars for a "tour." He got them all completely drunk and overcame censure by the home's authorities by soliciting reports from his other drinking buddies, the nurses. These men and women all proclaimed that the mood of the old folks had vastly improved after their excursion with administrator Christian who had been so selfless as to give up his lunch hour in service to the needy.

I would go to his house, sit with him in the kitchen, and listen to biographies of Provincetown's locals until the sun came up. Occasionally he would speak of his time on Broadway—bounce up from the chair and do a dance step that was short on expansive legwork because boxes surrounded the table and the Shih Tzus were always underfoot. This exhibition would be accomplished with long arms waving and flushed face invaded by pure ecstasy. The infantile teeth would gleam with spittle beneath the kitchen light and the eyes would blaze electric blue. And I was always struck by the fact, as he sat back down breathing heavily, that he had not a trace of regret or sadness in his laughing face. One friend had gone on to become the most successful playwright of his time, the other the most acclaimed actor of his generation—while Christian had come back to Provincetown to work in bars and hats, showing nothing less than exuberance for the life he had led.

One night I asked him why he had given up his great happy experience in New York at such an early age. Why had he quit the dance he had so obviously loved at the age of twenty-four? And his eyes smiled at the truth of his words. "Ahhh, my dear, I began to fall down onstage when I danced. You see, luv, I was tipsy a good deal of the time. There comes a day when you must make a choice. And I knew that as much as I loved to dance, there was really far more exhilaration to be found inside a jug." But then he held his hand up to shush me. The scanner was reporting the arrest of a drunken driver, and he jovially whispered, "A top administrator at the home. Considers me too flamboyant to work with the elderly. Has even tried to negotiate my removal." Defiance flared the nostrils, the head tilted back, and he looked down at me with maniacal eyes. "He shall never tarnish my dubious reputation again."

* * *

We had little in common regarding an appreciation of Provincetown's benefits so I decided to leave. I had had a lot of fun living there for five years, but I was beginning to see the place as a burial ground for all ambition outside the realm of booze. It was a very beautiful place, but it was also the world's largest wet bar thrust some forty miles out into the Atlantic. Even when I did not drink, the surrounding ocean gave my brains the sense of living inside an opium den. It was time to get back to reality.

And so early one morning, feeling like some kind of traitor, I dressed in a suit and tie and went to McMillan's parking lot to catch the bus to Boston. I was to be gone just for the day; I had a job interview. I stood there in the gray light of morning, nervous and full of doubt, and then Christian's car rolled up directly behind the bus that was just pulling in. He squeezed the brakes too hard and hats tumbled over the front seat, over his head, and against the windshield. He rushed out of the car, but so did the hats, and he had to chase a few across the parking lot. A gust of wind came up and sent the hats out across Cape Cod Bay, and then he went back to the car to get something.

When he stood before me, clutching a brown greasy bag, he was a bit breathless as he gushed, "Ahhhh, Gawd, luv! I'm glad I got here in time. I want things to go well for you in Boston and so I've packed you a healthy breakfast."

Suspiciously I said, "It's not stew, is it? You don't expect me to eat that stew on a moving vehicle."

"Special stew, luv. Not just stew. I made stew designed to bolster a man for his rise to the top in the city of Boston. I made squid valerian stew, darling! And you must eat it while you are being transported so the full nutritional effects will strike your intestines as you sally forth into the towers of greater Boston."

"Well thanks, Christian. I know how much time and effort goes into your stew so I really appreciate it. I have to get on the bus and you have to get to work. I'll call you later and let you know how the interview went." I took the bag. "What's in the thermos?"

"Bloodys, of course. Mixed with clam juice. You'll want a tall refreshing drink before the interview."

It was a three-hour ride on the bus from Provincetown to Boston, and I did not open the bag until I was fifteen minutes away from downtown's Park Square. When I surprised myself by deciding to have a bit of stew, it was not because I was hungry. I dared to eat the stew because I was homesick. I was very nervous about living in Boston, and the container of stew seemed to hold the essence of Provincetown's neuroticism. Suddenly, I felt ridiculously proud to have lived there, and I wanted a bowl of that crazy sea town in my stomach. And so I flipped off the top of the plastic container.

I looked down at the brown thick muck dotted with green peels, questioning the wisdom of my romantic impulse. And though I was not surprised at the aroma, there was an audible gasp of revulsion from my fellow passengers. The horrendous stink of squid laced with valerian and rotting limes had immediately filled the limited air space of the bus. Faces with grimaces of nausea turned to investigate the source of this devil worship mess. A voice croaked, "I gotta get off this bus," and it was the driver speaking.

He pulled over—when he could—to the side of the highway. He walked down the aisle, and I lifted my container so he could see. "Only my breakfast," I said. "No cause for alarm."

It was decided that the stew would rest in some grass alongside the highway, and we continued into Boston. But although Christian's culinary effort stayed behind like an offering left by the gates of the city, the expulsion of his living stew did nothing at all to dilute the lethal stink that lingered inside the bus.

I was totally spooked by this time. Leaving the demented lifestyle of Provincetown behind for the role of proper Bostonian seemed like an irresponsibly sober thing to do. The stench inside the bus had my psyche feeling as though trapped within a fisherman's drawn net.

I felt compelled to have a Christian-mixed Bloody Mary. So I unscrewed the cup top of the thermos, and it was instantly too late to contain the Bloody Mary, which was filled to the top of a neck that had a small piece broken off. Unscrew the tightly fitted cup and the drink inside overflowed the hand and, in my case, the white shirt, part of the tie, and crotch of the pants. My nerves shot, I poured from the thermos into the cup with trembling hands while the driver, moaning about his need to get to Park Square and evacuate the bus, careened down the highway. He took a curve at top speed, and I overpoured the cup. I looked down to watch more of the thick, dark red drink ooze down my white shirt on its way to the estuary of my crotch. I was saturated now with Christian's "tall refreshing drink"—heavy on the Worchestershire.

At Park Square, I rushed off the bus before the passengers could organize into a lynch mob. I ran a few blocks in search of a pay phone and called Christian. I expected his phone to ring a long time because usually he could not find the phone, which was located in the rubble of the living room. But miraculously he answered on one ring. And as he said hello in his basso profundo telephone voice, I remembered that he was supposed to be at work.

"It's me. I'm in trouble. But why are you home?"

"A Portuguese premonition, luv. I felt an overwhelming urge to stay here by the phone. So that I may be of assistance to you. In case you feel threatened. I am here to bolster your confidence. I shall not allow your mission to be aborted. Now lay it on me, luv. You're tense. What happened?"

"Well, I have a job interview in twenty minutes and I'm covered with Bloody Marys. I'm sweating heavily in that way you say is so healthy, and squid stew is pouring out of my glands. But the thermos Christian. You gave me a busted thermos!"

His voice held all the serenity of the bay on a rare windless afternoon. "So that was the reason for my Portuguese premonition. Ahhhh, luv, I must have fifty thermoses in my collection and I gave you the wrong one. I was operating with a splitting headache when I put your little breakfast together and well . . ."

"What am I gonna do now? What would you do?"

"Quite frankly, luv, I would not be in that uncivilized city to begin with. I have suffered vales of gastritis on past excursions to Boston."

"My interview, Christian! I can't come here to live unless I line up the job first."

"It is a ticklish situation, luv. I'm looking through my book to see who I could call. Who might be of help." And then that wind came up from out there where the bay meets the ocean and charged through the wires right into my ear. The gusting blow of an old sea captain roaring with laughter. "How mortifying for you, luv. You're prospective employer might get the idea you've been drinking!"

"Oh, man! I can't even get back on the bus. The driver will never let me back on. There's no chance he'd spend another three hours with me the way I smell. And he's it. He does the only return trip later and there is no other bus today."

"Ah, there! I've located the number."

"What number?"

"Larry's. He's the man who drove the bus. During the three-hour layover in Boston, there is a tavern he favors. I shall call him there and tell him to expect you later this afternoon."

"And he won't give me any trouble?"

"My dear, use your head. He is a bus driver drinking in a saloon. Months ago, it came over the scanner that the police had stopped his bus on the way into Provincetown. Weaving over the line. He's a local boy so they let him off easy, but naturally I had occasion to ask Larry about the encounter shortly thereafter. That's when he divulged the name of his Boston hangout. I shall have him paged immediately and arrange for him to welcome you on board for your return journey. And he shall greet you with all due respect or else the bus company shall receive a call from me loaded with tasty information about their driver. But before I get to work, I must tell you how sorry I am, luv. If I had made the drink properly then you would not sound so upset. I apologize. I'll make it up to you later this afternoon. Come straight to my house. Cocktails at about four? Dinner around midnight?"

"I feel like such a fail—"

"I plan a sweet and sour Oriental linguicia dish."

"I really shouldn't be living in that town."

"With potatoes and an exquisite squid gravy. And we shall dress. I have located a tuxedo for you with, I think, a precise fit. I simply have to remove a few wine stains. Yes! We dine with formality tonight! I shall tell the children of your imminent return. They will be thrilled. There to greet you at my door. And now I must call Larry. Feel free to bring a bottle of champagne on board your coach later, luv. A diversion for the repetition of a trip done twice in one day. Your driver, believe me, shall not raise an eyebrow. Goodbye, luv."

I was back in Provincetown by four that afternoon. And, of course, I rushed, smelling like a dead fish, to Christian's house so that I could get into a tuxedo in time for the cocktail hour.

And it was another year before I finally moved to Boston.

The Moon Again

"Yes!"—as they say. And even that was irritating me all day at work. The way everyone on television and so, of course, all the sheep who watch have incorporated this ebullient phrase of approval. "Yes!"—they bellow with orgasmic gusto. In recognition of all things great and small. For the completion of a major business deal. Or successful elimination inside the cubicle of a public rest room. "Yes!"—I hear them cry.

And "Cool!" Everything is cool. An expression that dates back nearly half a century to the Beat Generation of the 1950s. Back then it was said with a meditative, drawn-out sensuality as in—"Cooooollll." Today it is snapped off by an efficient whip of tongue without regard to the cooo sound. "Kowol!" Which had to have originated in California. Just as phrasing statements with the sound of a question is symptomatic of Western Wonderland. "And then I washed the car?" As though there is real doubt about the listener's capacity to understand. Or, "And then I washed the car, okay?" Signifying, "Are you with me so far?" Or approval sought for having washed the car.

"Timmy," says the five-year-old's lawyer, "we have a case against your father, okay? Abuse the day he spanked you for stabbing the cat?"

"Kowol!"

"We can send him up for five years?"

"Yes!"

These aggravating speech patterns flew through what was left of my riddled brain as I stood at the end of a dock in Hyannis Port. It was 2 a.m., and I was staring out at Nantucket Sound—a full moon above exposing ghostly boats and yachts tossing in the harbor.

It was a hot night in August, and I was not gazing out to sea in the middle of the night in a burst of poetic whimsy. I was out there because two bats had flown into the house I rented. They had come to call around midnight and then remained adamant in the face of my wish for eviction. They had entered through a bedroom window, and Joe and I concluded it was wise to let them stay the night. With some haste we shut the bedroom door behind us and withdrew to the couches in the living room.

Anyone who has ever been in a room with bats will understand why we forfeited our rightful habitat. Bats unnerve the bravest of people because they look like too many species rolled into one. They look like birds, flying rats, flying puppy dogs.

Within two hours I left the couch because it was too uncomfortable, and I walked two blocks to the harbor. I don't know why, but as I gazed at a Cape Cod panorama of perfection, I began to reflect upon things like "Kowol" and "Yes!" But not for long. Because I soon remembered the snub I had received from my neighbor on the previous day.

I had been walking up my driveway late in the afternoon while the old man had been working on the sprinkler system of his lawn, which adjoins my property. Down on one shaky knee, he had looked up to see me and then quickly looked down again. Just so he could pretend ignorance of my presence. Executed this age-old ploy just so he wouldn't have to say "Hi." And I knew that this blatant exhibition of snobbery was simply because I *rented* in Hyannis Port while he *owned*. And then, too, although High-Anus Port had the reputation of a sophisticated community full of worldly types like the Kennedys, it was still a conservative village. I mean, if you were anyone at all, you never mentioned the Kennedys. My neighbor could well be of the Republican turn of mind that disavowed the presence of two men living alone together. If they could try to ignore the liberal Kennedys, it served to reason that one of their clique would not find it hard to become all wrapped up in a sprinkler system as I passed by to join my queer little buddy.

And even though my neighbor suffered from Alzheimer's disease, let's be honest, rude is rude. Homophobic is homophobic. His sister-in-law could relate all the stories she cared to tell about how the old man was always forgetting who he was. How he had, for example, one day flown off to Bismarck, North Dakota, for no apparent reason and had had to be returned home by medical authorities. This did not change the possibility that Alzheimer's victims were open to homophobia.

Standing out there looking at the millionaires' yachts, I became more upset than ever by the snub of the preceding afternoon. And I was forced to wonder if the bats had been sent by an avenging angel to punish my enemies.

The old man kept his windows open at night. And on the side of the house, one window lacked a screen. A replica of the situation that had allowed air passage into my bedroom. Now if I could find a way to catch my bats—maybe trap them in a large box—I could transfer them at night to the old man's house. Afford the horrifying creatures a few steps up on the Hyannis Port social ladder.

But then, thrilled by the brilliance of this idea for righteous retribution, I had to go and irritate the hell out of myself. For I found myself spinning around to face the wealthy homes that ringed the harbor. "YES!" I shouted. "LEAD A CHARGE OF BATS RIGHT INTO THE OLD GEEZER'S HOME! OH, MAN! KOWOL!"

I had to take a minute to collect myself. And then I wondered how I could maneuver the bats into a box. Would I suffer the furies of rabies if I got bitten? Did rabies shots still hurt a lot, as they were known to do when I was a kid? How expensive were the rabies shots? And I turned bitter because I had to actually stop and consider the cost of terrorism while that sonuvabitch next door was so goddamn rich he could afford to fly all over the fucking country for absolutely no reason at all.

Now (as the old man suddenly vanished on the smoke of my fiery brain). These bats. I might have a real problem back at the house because I was sure I had read somewhere that they were social creatures. Didn't they call to each other by sonar? Get all comfy in a new abode and immediately start sending out the invitations?

By this time, probably all the relatives and freeloading friends had moved into my bedroom. Living it up and hanging upside down from the crossbeams up near the ceiling. Chatting about the night's events in that high-pitched faggy screech of theirs.

I stood there mulling over this dreadful scenario when tiny stage hands trooped across the stage of my mind to change the set. And I could see one wall of the living room. I remembered the fascinating encounter with a wall switch that had occurred before the bats had arrived.

I had been reading an Elvis Presley cookbook in the living room when the bulb of the lamp went out. They always do during full moons so I cannot say I was surprised. But while I was engaged in changing the lightbulb I had occasion to examine the wall switch. Because the wall switch halfway up the wall was home to the outlet for the plug of the lamp. Entertaining a life-long fear of execution through bulb replacement I had had to extract the plug and reenter the plug during operations. And in so doing, I noted that the wall switch covering was firmly riveted to the wall by four healthy young screws.

Not very long after I had survived the changing of the bulb in my lamp, I turned off the light to go to bed—unknowingly headed for a fateful and potentially disease-threatening encounter with bats. But before I left the living room, my eyes fell upon the wall switch and I realized that the covering was loose!

I wish I could report that I was quick in my analysis of what was happening inside the living room, but I abhor ego enlargement, and I must confess to having been not wholly attentive. In fact, I moved all the way into the bedroom where Joe was staring mysteriously out the unscreened window before there was the clap of thunder in my consciousness.

Oh, fuck no! The wall switch covering!

I did not run back into the living room. I couldn't run. I was too heavy with the weight of implication.

But when I did find myself back in front of the wall, it was there right before my eyes. The dismantling of a wall switch cover by the moon. The cover was hanging loose from the wall where a half hour before it had been tightly screwed. And as I stood there, my eyes beheld the awesome spectacle of one screw falling to the floor.

I made a tough decision right away. Which was that nothing could be done. No purpose served by alarming Joe. What for? We were within the force of an insidious magnetism that practiced its craft within the atmosphere. How does one pack up and leave the atmosphere?

Like a soldier possessed by fear of land mines, I tiptoed carefully back into the bedroom. As I got under the covers, the last words I heard Joe say as he innocently fell asleep were, "What a beautiful moon tonight. Shining right in through the window."

I believe it was at the stroke of midnight when I experienced the fan of air across my dozing face. When I opened my eyes to observe the second pass above my head, I cannot say I was unimpressed, but I was not taken by surprise either. There may have been a white-knuckled grip of the covers, but I distinctly recall my brain's calculating summary of the situation. There was a military precision to my reaction. First, I informed myself of the presence of a bat in the room. Lying perfectly still, I numbered the enemy at two. During a third reconnaissance flight above my face, I noted how these celestial mammals resembled the designs for flying machines drawn by Leonardo da Vinci. Then I performed a cooly rational prognosis of intent—their objective.

My first consideration was, of course, that they had been sent by homophobic maniacs (provoked by the old man next door?). I watched them circle the room and scrutinized for canisters of anthrax and smallpox disease strapped to their bodies. Second, I confess that I had to line up Joe for suspicion of collusion. There was no other recourse. I mean, the man had stood there staring out the screenless window before going to bed. Had he sent up a flare? Was there a hidden sonar device in his jaws? He could have been bitten by a Manchurian bat as a child and programmed for this night over thirty years ago. I looked at his sleeping face on the pillow next to mine, thinking how we never really know anyone. Fourteen years together, and I was lying there next to him speculating upon his role in a plan to inflict smallpox disease upon my person (knowing that his own immunity had to have come by contract to collude).

Well, all right. My own love was large enough to accept any defect in Joe's character by this time. And I lay there for a few more minutes, wondering if there was any sexual potential involved with this new insight into his character. You did that after fourteen years. Even the discovery of murderous impulse makes its way onto the list of techniques for innovative sex.

It was time to spring into action, and I leaped from the bed, while with one brisk and athletic swipe of the hand I brought the blanket with me. Whirled this blanket with all the force of a lifetime's resentment. A human helicopter was I, with blades of cloth atwirl above my head. "Get the fuck outta here, you homo-phobic Irish-American biased Middle Eastern bastard!" I screamed. And would most definitely have snared them with that blanket and then squeezed the life out of them with my bare hands. For I am essentially an unstoppably heroic man. But then Joe woke up and had another idea. He jumped from the bed and with just two exciting strides was gone from the room. And no longer having family to protect, I thought I might follow suit.

But it was not over just yet.

I paused at the door. I watched the two of them. Witnessed the malicious temerity of these midnight harlequins as they relaxed into their new quarters so quickly. Observed them as they obtru-sively took possession of the crossbeam and then hung upside down—their way of saying "Shove it up your ass" to the bona fide lessee who stood fuming in the door.

And then.

Retaliation for having greeted them with propelling blanket. A purposeful glare of eyes directed at me from the upside-down shrunken heads before I could manage to close the door. My head snapped back as the blast of sonar ripped right through my skull, resulting in the headache I suffered through the rest of the mias-mic night. And it was this injury inflicted by the vengeful light of a full moon (bolts thrown at earth by a moon god still petulant over Americans playing golf on his turf) that maimed my sleep on the sagging living room couch.

And now I stood on this dock in the harbor of Hyannis Port and nearly wept with indignation because I remembered what my next-door neighbor's grandchildren had tried to do only one week before. I stood there and hot tears rolled down my cheeks. That they could actually conspire with such incredibly evil intent to hurt this harmless and stricken old feller.

He had flown away again—this time to Casper, Wyoming. And the two boys—college students—had placed an Open House sign in front of Grandfather's house to attract buyers. They were attempting to haul down a hefty cash advance payment on the house while Grandad roamed around Casper. And when I learned of this exploit, I had simply nodded my head—sage acknowledgment of history's repercussions. For I knew they were Nixonian babies.

You see, they had been conceived not long after the decayed cusp of the Nixon years. They were a product of a pestiferous generation who, even though they had despised Nixon at the time, had gestating within themselves the seeds of Nixonia. For many subsequent years, all children born to this pathetic generation were reared in the spirit of a people designated to one day own an entire nation full of fraudulent used car lots.

These particular Nixonian vipers failed with their noxious scheme. They were stopped by a local realtor who happened to drive by the house, saw the sign, and, knowing the old man, decided to do some checking. Since he was of the generation that came of age during the seventies, I am sure he checked into the viability of the Nixonian rodents' plan before deeming it un-workable. Then he pounced, energized by considerations of fi-nancial reward.

So maybe the old man had not meant to snub me after all. Maybe he was simply brokenhearted and distressed by betrayal. And there was the Alzheimer's thing too.

Thinking about it, maybe he was some kind of genius. All that traveling. Wasn't it possible he journeyed in search of vibration zones in various parts of the country? He was not at all mindless. He traveled to get his messages.

But those scumbag grandchildren and their appalling greed! Oh, how I would enjoy seeing the two of them stretched upon a medieval rack, wheel turned to the tune of their beloved Smashing Pumpkins. Bones separated in syncopation with the beat of drums.

Of course, it had to be the two kids who had released the bats into my bedroom.

Well, maybe not both of them.

The dark-haired one was cute in a way. Nice ass.

But I'll bet the malignant little roach would nail me for harassment if I so much as executed a peripheral cruise.

I was getting weary of living as I stood on the dock. It was close to 3 a.m., and I watched my domineering dog as he trotted purposefully down the length of the dock to fetch me home.

I must have left the front door open and the dog, Bob, always eyes me with suspicion during full moons. He worries about my behavior, and at the age of twelve—after all these years—I am forced to conclude that he may know what he is barking about.

And he was barking now as he came toward me. Those irritating short yaps, "C'mon, dude, let's go home. C'mon now, move it, dude." Another word I hate—dude. Which even my dog uses.

My gaze fell upon him as he stood in front of me and so I chanced to realize I was naked. Had forgotten to dress before leaving the house.

I let Bob gently take my hand in his mouth and lead me, bewildered, across the moon-smashed dock. Hoping for redemption. Dreaming of monasteries in which to reside.

Marilyn: The Last Performance

Marilyn.
Incomparable Marilyn.
The fuse of life.
She was Hollywood when she danced. Not of the Russian school. She wasn't pretentious. She was ours. America at its best. Shirley MacLaine comes to mind.

On her good nights, a pirouette was composed of grace indigenous to her class, and yet there was a sinister quality in the highly disciplined set of expression. She had the most marvelous jowls. She would baffle those in the audience who were attending her performance for the first time.

Even when it all went wrong—when the drinks registered upon her face like buckled tide marks on the shore—she was still Marilyn. I watched her final performance with the same sense of tense history as the night I saw Callas sing at Carnegie Hall for the last time. Because she was the end of her line, you see. In so many ways she resembled us, the oldest generation. Even when the pirouette became a lunge, even when she landed out cold on the floor, she was still the poetess of our lost dreams.

To see her on that rainy afternoon laid out in the Budweiser box, flowers up and down the bar, the room packed with devotees, made one feel that one's youth had faded irreversibly. That at seventy-eight this fan's heart might never pirouette again.

And when I followed with the small cortege up the hill in the pouring rain, I thought of Marilyn's place among other brilliant souls associated with the metaphor of an inclement day.

Ava Gardner in a Spanish cemetery—the perfect machine-driven rain falling with such dramatic effect upon the early grave of the Barefoot Countessa.

The transcendental Audrey in *Breakfast at Tiffanys*—standing there in that filthy New York City alley, the soaking rain somehow enhancing the magnitude and clarity of her breathtaking eyes. Clutching a drenched cat to her bosom and contemplating a life with George Peppard. Soon after she was in *The Nun's Story*.

The night before, I had seen Marilyn alive for the last time, and she had reminded me of that other Marilyn in *The Misfits*. She had already drunk a quart of Kahlúa and there came a moment, during this last dance, when she began to look somewhat strange. It occurred just before she fell to the floor for the final act. Suddenly, with a premonition of impending doom, I thought of the close-up on Monroe's face during the climactic scene of her *last* picture. Our Marilyn's facial expression was exactly the same as the other Marilyn's projection of horror when she finally realizes that all the lovely horses on the ranch will soon find their next life experienced inside the confines of cans destined for dog food.

I am at that age when the great ironic connections are becoming readily apparent.

Up on top of the hill, Harold shoveled out the grave. He wore a look of perplexity while the rain frustrated his attempt to keep mud and water from inundating Marilyn's final resting place. Tall and thin but for a protruding belly, a hundred keys jangling on his hip, the prominent awesome log that he said he had to keep tied by rope to his thigh—the sixty-one-year-old Harold performed his second tragic task of the day.

He was only sixty-one, but he had already enjoyed two careers in his life. He had grown up in a family that had owned a funeral parlor, and until he reached forty he was a most successful embalmer. He then realized a need to creatively extend himself and for a while considered crematoriums or, as he put it, "the shake-and-bake field." But instead he decided to move out here to Provincetown, to cook in his own restaurant, exchanging the idea of one kind of oven for another. He teamed up with his lover, Jason, to open an establishment that had a fair-sized lounge as well as dining room, and it is here that Marilyn ascended to stardom. Jason, who had over half a century of experience in lounges, assumed command of the bar.

Watching Harold now—involved with the labor that I knew he associated with the more mundane end of death's production line—I thought of his earlier ordeal. He had decided to come out of retirement from his first career, had decided that his own loving hands would embalm Marilyn. And perform an autopsy too, since he had witnessed many in the old days when youthful exuberance had drawn him into morgues and autopsy rooms to make more well rounded his education. And although his decision must have invoked absolutely enthralling memories of the past, there was sorrow on his knitted brow when, work completed, he brought Marilyn down in the Budweiser box to lay her on top of the bar.

He guessed he was a little rusty, he told us. He could not get one of Marilyn's legs to fold as comfortably as the other three. And so Marilyn rested in the Budweiser box with three legs folded peacefully at the joints and the left front leg sticking straight up in the air. Smiling ruefully, Harold remarked that the uplifted leg might be an indication that Marilyn intended someday to dance her way right up from the grave.

I stood there brimming with admiration for the trooper in the man, a spirit he had no doubt imparted to Marilyn in times of professional distress. This man had a clientele to cook for as well as a duty to perform on Marilyn. And he had accomplished both simultaneously. Had, in a manner of speaking, carved in the light of two occupations. He had done the autopsy upstairs on the kitchen table while preparing the evening's cuisine. With steely stoicism, he had surrounded himself with pots and pans—chickens, steaks, and the cadaver. To center himself he had stationed a bottle of Cutty Sark on the table and played his favorite classical music, Wagner's "Ride of the Valkyries." Imagine the concentration of the man holding sway over two arts at once—the culinary and the dissective. A dash of cooking sherry here, the fine-tuned probing of a liver there. And through it all the memories. Ah, the memories! The ghost of his subject arrayed in the pots before his eyes, up and pirouetting across the long kitchen table, spinning above the chops and baby peas and the sundry vitals of her former existence.

The bar in which Marilyn had been laid out was called The Marilyn Room. The walls were yellow and graced with the largest collection of Marilyn Monroe photographs to be found on all of Cape Cod. Interspersed with the great legend were pictures of our Marilyn, most of them action stills of her dance. There would be, for instance, the famous shot of Norma Jean in *The Seven-Year Itch*—standing on the subway grating, dress blown high. And right next to that classic hung our little football Marilyn atwirl in the air, her adorable gangsterlike face showing two teeth hooked over the lower lip. And on and on. An exhibition of high-water marks in show business history.

While Harold had been busy upstairs with scissors and knife, needle and thread, Jason had been holding the fort downstairs at the bar. This was Jason's forte. He had been holding the fort at various bars for most of his seventy-five years, and no one did it better. He was a tiny man at 5'2" and very proud of his full head of hair—a perfectly combed brush cut, chestnut colored with rather bright red (or orange?) highlights. Another outstanding feature was the large brown unblinking eyes. They seemed petrified in his masklike face; Jason had a highly dignified catatonic look to him.

The bar was raised two feet up from the floor on a platform, and if you sat at one of the cocktail tables, only Jason's head was visible behind the bar. This provoked a disquieting effect, for Jason always paced up and down the length of the bar whenever he was not pouring drinks. And all that could be viewed from the cocktail tables was a frozen face floating ever so slowly to and fro, with an equally slow mechanical movement of glass to lips. More than one Marilyn fan had noted Jason's resemblance to a target moving on the treadmill of a shooting gallery.

When Marilyn lay on top of the bar and Jason stood behind, I gazed with fondness upon the stillness of face the two shared. I remembered the past nights of glory. The enormous bottle of Kahlúa that stood on the right side of the bar, visible to the entire room. The bottle was synonymous with the dance. For if one purchased a shot of Kahlúa for fifteen dollars, it was like buying a ticket to the show. Jason would tell the star to dance, and after Marilyn leaped and pirouetted, she would come to your table for her Kahlúa.

But her life was not completely a bed of roses. After Marilyn's fame had spread among residents and tourists, the inevitable rumors started. Just as they do with any star in a country that enjoys placing mortals on a pedestal just to have the vicious fun of tearing them down. There were unfounded stories of scandal in the family. It was said that she was not really a blue-line pug—that her mother had run off with a pit bull, the offspring of which was Marilyn. She was rumored to have once worked as a bouncer at cockfights. Some said they had seen her dance in a club of ill repute where Marilyn would pick up coins with her . . .

We had been waking Marilyn for about an hour at the bar when Jason asked for the results of the autopsy. Since by this time the bar had filled with Marilyn's fans, Harold saw fit to whisper his report. With the pride of an old retired baseball player who had come back to hit one out on Old Timer's Day, he said, "Either cirrhosis, heart disease, or pancreatic cancer. God! It made me feel young again, boys. Working on her like that. I put everything in a doggie bag and threw it in the incinerator."

Jason thought over the report for a minute. And when he replied, his lips moved but the rest of his face had all the expression of a duck hunter's decoy. "In other words, she was partially cremated."

"You could say that," said Jason.

There were a good six or seven grieving fans packed into the bar, but I was the only one who accompanied Harold, Jason, and Marilyn up the hill to the gravesite. It was to be a very private burial, and now I must painfully relate the reason for my attendance.

I am a footnote to the history of a show business queen. I occupy a most dubious place in the fate that befell Marilyn. When all the accounts are settled in the ledger of her career, I shall be listed as a debit. Yes, a debit! Damned forever as a doddering old debit!

For it was none other than this decrepit debit who gave to Marilyn her last drink of Kahlúa.

It was late last night when I purchased the Kahlúa, and Harold, serving as cocktail waiter, brought the drink to my ringside table. I remember the scene vividly. The high spirits of the audience. Marilyn with that sultry crooked grin, leaning against the bar. Jason's disembodied head, the stunned look to the unblinking eyes. The way Harold limped over to me with the drink while others at the surrounding tables stared, as always, at the enormous log draped down his thigh.

I had asked Harold why he was limping and he explained—loud enough for everyone to hear. "I got a rope burn." And grinned rather sexily, even though his teeth resided in a wine glass behind the bar. "I gotta control the thing somehow or other. Especially when I'm working down here with Jason." And there was polite laughter at the surrounding tables and a smattering of applause while Jason stared, transfixed, into infinite space.

It was Harold who cued the star on this occasion, and Marilyn, reddened eyes upon the Kahlúa on my table, came out to her space in the middle of the floor. Harold hit the tape button. *Swan Lake* majestically filled the room, and Marilyn tried to lift from her feet. I could see her making the effort to spring upward, but she never left the floor. She simply stood on her hind legs moving up and down on her toes. It was then that I saw the look of Norma Jean in *The Misfits*. A sudden horrified expression just before she pushed upward, yet again only to fall backward onto the floor. And then she slowly rolled over and crawled to my feet and beseeched me with desperate eyes for the drink. And I complied; I set the drink down on the floor even though, in truth, I had not received fifteen dollars worth of dance.

She drank it down quickly and then looked up at me. I think she might have been trying to convey her good-byes, for her eyes signaled a sense of departure just before they rolled back in her head. And then our little football shuddered once and fell backward, the second time within minutes. She never got up again. The curtain had come down for the final time.

I went home deeply troubled last night. A nagging in the soul. There were formless questions in my mind. As though I should be rethinking the kind of life I led. But I could not even make articulate the question, let alone seek the answer. I sat in my rocking chair, and Isadora climbed up to lie in my lap. She is always a tonic for me whenever I despair of living, and smiling down at her, tracing the little liver spots on her paws with my fingers, I dozed. At least I had done something right in my life when I had refused Isadora her wish to enter through the portals of show business.

* * *

There is a lovely view of Cape Cod Bay from the hill behind the restaurant. The hill slopes down to Commercial Street, and across the street begins the beach. While Harold tangled with the grave that kept filling with water, I stood there in the rain talking to Jason. All of us wore our yellow slickers.

"Did you see the headstone?" he whispered.

"No, I haven't," I said.

"Behind you. We'll set it in the ground when the ground's more solid."

I turned to see the small stone lying flat in the grass, inscription side up.

MARILYN

Feb. 15, 1997-Aug. 15, 1997
My mother thanks you
My father thanks you
And I thank you

"Yankee Doodle Dandy," I said.

"Yes. Jimmy Cagney's line. You know, she always reminded me of Cagney."

"I thought the smile was Bogart's."

"Depended on the time of day you saw her. She was so many people really. Makes you realize. You never really know anyone."

"God, I wish she had had children."

"Well, I don't think she'd mind if I told you. She was a lesbian, and she had problems with that."

"Ahhh. Well, Jason, I have to tell you. I did wonder. But why the problems? When we're all queer as three-dollar bills out here."

"I'll tell you something else. She was in love with your Isadora."

"But Isadora's been seeing John Travolta for months."

"John Travolta was a front for Marilyn's closet problems. The girls used John Travolta."

Harold had left the casket in a toolshed a few feet from the plot when he realized the problem he had on his hand with the rain. Now he came over to us holding the closed Budweiser box in his hands. "I'm going to try and bury her," he said in a knotted tone of voice—a man attempting to keep himself together.

"We did remember to put the bottle of Kahlúa in with her, didn't we?" Jason asked.

"Done. I'm just hoping the box holds together. It's soaked, and you know her leg never did fold properly."

He turned and placed the box down gently into the grave where it floated and bobbed in the water. Then he began to shovel mud on top. The rain seemed to be falling even harder than before.

Jason whispered, "You believe in a hereafter? I sometimes think I'm already there."

"Jason, I have to tell you something. My Isadora is not a lesbian. Dachshunds are never lesbians. Have you ever heard of a lesbian dachshund?"

"Well, I must say that it's a pretty sweeping statement to make when you imply that there are no lesbian dachshunds."

But then Harold joined us, and using the lexicon of his youth, he said with great dignity, "She is interred." And then turned to look out over the bay. Which seemed like the dramatically correct thing to do. Jason and I also turned to gaze soulfully upon the stormy water.

And it was then that Harold broke down. He had held together magnificently through all of the long day, and now he sank to his knees uttering a strangled cry. I looked at Jason, but he was gone—the unblinking eyes far out at sea, face fossilized. Harold had his face buried in his hands and he was speaking, but I could not make out a word.

Suddenly there was a movement along my peripheral vision (which is excellent for my age), and I turned my head. "My God!" I yelled, "Boys! Look!"

Harold jerked his head to see and then sprang to his feet. Jason's straight-ahead gaze never wavered.

Marilyn's casket was floating down the hill on a river of rain.

"We've got to do something!" I screamed.

But Harold put his hand on my shoulder. "No. Don't you see? She wants to be buried at sea. She's on her way to the sea."

Jason actually spoke then, staring directly ahead, a small flutter of lips. "A Cecil B. DeMille Production. Charlton Heston should be here."

"This is her great comeback," said Harold reverently. "I should have known she would do it her way."

And so we just stood there and let her go. The casket coasted down the hill as though navigated by a willful mystical inhabitant. I could see a car coming down Commercial Street just as the casket approached the sidewalk, and it looked for a moment as though this divine and inspirational vision would end as just a common traffic accident. But then the Budweiser box was jarred as it came over the steep curb, and the drenched flaps of the box were burst apart by an inner force. That stubborn leg which would not fold shot through the box, jolting Marilyn upright in the box at the same time.

If the driver of the car had not seen the box through the heavy rain, he was most aware of it now. Marilyn reincarnated as traffic cop—the leg straight out—"Halt!"

A screech of brakes. One can only speculate what thoughts passed through the driver's mind as he beheld the stern demeanor of our Marilyn, teeth hooked over the lower lip and commanding leg aloft.

As the car swerved and smashed into the telephone pole in front of the restaurant, Harold and I had our arms in the air, hands waving. "Good-bye, Marilyn! Godspeed!"

Still in the stream of water from the hill, the box bounced across the street and over the sands of beach. When it reached the shore, it caught the first wave and she was on her way.

The three of us stood atop the hill watching, gladness in our hearts. Even Jason was somewhat animated when he said, "Hope the Kahlúa didn't fall out of the box."

Just a trifle annoyed by the sound of sirens in the street, we could keep her in sight for a little while longer. Away she sailed, sitting straight up in the box, the leg pointing toward the horizon. As though commanding the waves to take her toward the next performance.

Manifest Destiny Magazine

The Secret Invasion/Cuban Gay Army Attacks Key West

Jackie Hernandez:

It happened the year Key West became a nation. What do you call it? Secession? I was living there at the time. I am from a beautiful little country: Uruguay. Though it is not so beautiful that I would take it over the air-conditioned Key West and Miami. So far as the Cuban problem goes, I do not take sides. All the same to me with all the secret deals the little people know nothing about. I am a female impersonator. I am in the show business, and at the time we are speaking about, I was working in a club on Duval called the Pink Python. Also, since my career had not yet taken off, I was working part-time as a room service waitress in a downtown hotel. One day a very powerful man took the penthouse of the hotel. He was supposed to be the richest man in Florida, maybe in all the United States, for all I know. His name was Ricco Trashista. And along about one o'clock on the day he checked in, he was taken hostage by a woman I worked with named Vera Verboten. Her hero was Fidel Castro. She wanted 400 million dollars from Trashista, and she wanted passage to Cuba where she would give the money to Fidel to improve his country. She was from Germany, so she was crazy, of course. But you know, I did not think any of this was such a big deal. Key West still had a Florida mentality and kidnappings happened all the time. Everyone was used to terrorism. Who cares about these things except for the rich, who are always being threatened, and who cares about the rich? But the TV cameras are in the hotel lobby and they are making the Trashista kidnapping a big thing, while I am on my way out the door to keep an appointment at the beauty parlor because I am going to give myself a new image. The woman I admire most in the whole history of the world is Jacqueline Onassis, whose first name I took for myself when I decided to become a show business legend. You can keep Eva Peron. In spite of what they say, I never thought Eva Peron knew how to dress. Jacqueline, now she was another story when she was First Lady and had her hair in the fashionable little wings that stuck out of her head. And I loved the short little dresses, though not short enough to be cheap, and most of all I loved the pillbox hats she wore. I may not even be five feet tall, and it is true I am on the heavy side, but I saw myself bringing back the great Jacqueline style. I would perform and bring Jacqueline back to life at the Pink Python four nights a week. And so I am all punched out of the hotel and on my way to the beauty parlor where I have a friend who says he can help to make my eyes look far apart just like Jacqueline's. I have already ordered the wig with the petite wings and the pill-box hat. I am almost out the door when the police are asking me if I will bring lunch to Vera Verboten who is holding Ricco Trashista hostage in the penthouse. Vera has specifically ordered that I bring the lunch, and the police want me to do this and then report back to them to tell if Trashista is still in one piece. So I say, "Oh, okay," if the police chief will call the beauty parlor and explain to them that I will be late. He says he will do this and I bring up Vera's lunch, which is knockwurst and sauerkraut and Alsace reisling wine and streusel and Starbucks coffee. Against the wishes of the police chief, I have also brought the bill be-cause this is all very annoying to me. I enter the living room of the penthouse and crazy Vera is in her glory. She walks around with what I am later told is a Tec 9 gun, which can kill many people in about two seconds. She told me she bought this thing in a thrift shop. Trashista is seated at a table and Vera cheerfully tells me to watch while she tortures him. She is acting like a silly schoolgirl. On the table is a suitcase full of money belonging to Trashista. He had told Vera that this money was to be a donation for a center for the homeless, but she did not believe him, and neither did I. No one in Key West or Florida cares about the homeless. They would rather shoot the homeless than give them a home in this expensive territory. Vera, acting disgustingly girlish for a woman her age (she says forty-five—hah!—lines over her mouth like the handles of pliers and yet she says forty-five), says to me, "Watch this, Jackie." And holding the gun with one hand she pulls out a large stack of hundred-dollar bills, places the money in front of Trashista, and lights all this cash with a cigarette lighter that is childproof and so takes five minutes for it to work. But soon enough, the money is in flames and Trashista begins to scream in agony. Vera takes another stack and burns these under his eyes also, and Trashista is screaming, "Nooo! Noooo! Please!" and tears are running down his face, and then he becomes unconscious from the pain. And then Vera gets down to business with me. She says that she will pay me one million dollars of the ransom if I will contact a man in Key West by the name of Alex Delamooche. This man has connections to Fidel, and Vera says she can trust him to make arrangements for the transfer of money and to get her safely over to Cuba where she will live happily ever after working in the sugarcane fields. Now! I must tell you honestly that for a million dollars, I would suck the farts out of a monkey's ass. So of course I agree immediately and tell her I will go and find this Alex Delamooche who, as we speak, is my current husband and manager. But just for her own benefit, I also tell Vera she is crazy. I tell her that there is very poor air-conditioning in Cuba; it is a very great mistake to live there. I fought my way into the United States from little Uruguay because no country in the world has air-conditioning such as you will find in the United States. I told Vera to think carefully about what a move to Cuba truly meant. What it meant was a life of limp, lifeless hair such as she could not even imagine. I tried to make her realize this, but she would not listen and so I said, "Okay." I would do the job for a million, meanwhile thinking that now I can realize my dreams of buying my own club which will showcase so many of my talents that have gone unrecognized in Key West. I will call my place THE CLUB JACQUELINE ONASSIS. I will greatly further my career in the show business. After all, my life is show business. But I have no idea the tangled web I am tangling . . . however the expression goes. I have no idea I am now a player on a course that can lead to the first biological war. A war that will pit gay man against gay man, literally. The great secret war between Cuba and Key West! But! Before I can tell you of this great historical confrontation, I must have money. I have not yet received the check that we agreed upon. I have stories to tell of the mysterious gay spray biological weapon that will curl your hair but, Señor, really! Please! The check! I do not come so cheap. Would the great Jacqueline do this interview for nothing? Jacqueline never made a move in her life for nothing, and I am the same. I have the inside information on the female impersonator Maria Gomez who is Fidel Castro's illegitimate and long-unrecognized son. But I cannot say one more word without the check. I do not speak for nothing.

General Le Maize:

I was an advisor to the president of the United States at the time. Latin American Affairs. Now, to be frank, I never understood the deal that allowed Key West to secede. A lot of us in the government at the time were quite taken aback. I mean, how does a great and powerful nation lose a jewel of an island like Key West to a bunch of goddamn hairdressers? I'll tell you one thing. It would never happen on my goddamn watch. I would have blown those fucking fairies right out of the water before they could ever get control of that island. But from what I hear, the president was playing politics with the guy who was Mayor down there, Vincente Rollovo, the same guy who picked up all the marbles and went on to become president of Key West Nation, or Queer Nation, as those despicable slime pots down there call it. Now I am aware that the president of the United States denies that Cuba ever attacked Key West. Denies it to this day. And so does Fidel Castro deny it. Interesting, huh? How these two men finally find something to agree upon. But let me assure you. I was on the island when the war broke out, and I am just one of many witnesses. It was a confusing situation, but it did happen. First reports said that the Cubans landing on the island were just another version of Castro's Mariel boat lift. Another attempt to unload undesirables. In this case—the reasoning was that Castro was getting rid of 500 homosexuals. But then a subsequent report said there was evidence that the Cubans were armed with biological weapons. And that they were all naked! Five hundred Cuban soldiers, naked as jay birds, storming the beach at Key West with biological weapons! If you ask me, President Rollovo was in a position to be the first leader in the history of the world to stop a war simply by arresting the invading force for lewd and lascivious behavior. But then we arrive at the central issue. Would Rollovo's militia—queer to a man—actually either arrest or, if need be, fight against 500 naked young Latinos? In regard to an answer, I must tell you of one strategic advantage the Cubans had against the Key West Militia. A U.S. satellite equipped with cameras just happened to photograph the terrain of battle that night, and so we later learned through computerization of the photographs that every Cuban man advancing up the beach that historic and infamous night was in possession of an erection. And Castro knew his enemy well. He picked his own troops well. Most of the men were so unusually . . . constructed . . . that it was hardly necessary to blow up the photos to detect the detail. The Cuban anatomical advantage was that obvious. Even from outer space.

Pedro Gomez:

I am writing a book about the assassination of my sister, Maria Gomez, so I cannot tell you much for free. She was my half sister. Or half brother, though I believe she would rather be known as my half sister. Although she did identify herself as the blood son instead of blood daughter of Fidel Castro. Whichever, Fidel was her father—blood father. The fifty-one-year-old son Fidel never wanted the world to know about just because he wore women's clothing and maybe also because Maria once dated Che Guevara. Which my publisher told me not to talk about because it is a big selling point for my book, which will be published in the fall. Maria's career in show business was not going anywhere in Cuba, which is why she asked for asylum when she managed to bring her nightclub act to the Pink Python in Key West Nation. But then her career was cut short. She was assassinated by the Key West gay right the night of her Pink Python opening. And after she was shot, the unexpected happened. Her father's long-imprisoned love for his son came pouring out. Fidel's heart was broken and for that reason he invaded Key West. Because his beloved son was murdered by Key West gay right-wingers. Shot to smithereens during her opening number at the Pink Python on Duval Street. Shot to smithereens but—and here is what you will read in my book due out in the fall—the order to kill Maria came from much higher up than anyone knew at the time. About as high as you can go! I will also tell of the biological weapons and of the spray that almost ruined my life. Me, a devout Catholic with a wife and fourteen children. How I was shot with the spray and started leaving my home at night and my wife Serafina and my fourteen children. I was so sick with the spray that I would go out at night like a vampire to feed on the sexual organs of men. And then come back home to Serafina and my children and kneel with them in prayer that I might rid myself of this horrible obsession. One night they found me choking to death in the street because in my great obsession I had eaten the ring off a man's member. I lay in the gutter half dead with this ring lodged in my throat, my hands clutching the rosary. And I have not even mentioned my marriage to Harry Snit, who will never, as long as he lives, learn how to treat a woman right.

Rick Spittle:

I own the Pink Python, and I'm familiar with a lot of the high rollers who pass through Key West. I didn't know Trashista personally, but I knew plenty about him and when he was taken hostage by the Kraut, I knew there was gonna be big trouble. I knew he donated heavily to the president of the United States and I knew that he was involved with payoffs to Castro for the prospective sale of land in Cuba once relations normalized with the United States. When trade resumed, Trashista was gonna be the first man outta the gate. His real problem when he was taken by the Kraut was how much she knew about his deals with Castro. Because Castro was her hero, who could tell what she would do if she found out Fidel was not what he appeared to be? She was a pretty unstable kid, from what I understood, and both the American president and Castro had a lot to worry about if the Kraut got Trashista to talk. If he really talked, she might shoot him and then that's the end of golden goose. But much worse than that, the Kraut could tell the world about Trashista's funding of the supposed two archenemies—the American and Cuban presidents. As for Maria Gomez, I never really believed she was Castro's son, but it was good PR for her engagement at my club. But I began to get edgy when some of these political types around Key West began to put out the word that Gomez was actually an informer for Castro. They said she had a history of informing on gay radicals in Cuba, that she was responsible for their imprisonment.

Harry Snit:

I work on the staff of *The Nation's Nose* magazine and I was down in Key West vacationing. I was under a lot of pressure at the time because I hadn't come up with a story for *The Nose* in too long a time. So I'm in my hotel room one night, and even though I'm supposed to be on vacation, I got all these photos the magazine sent me spread out all over the floor. I'm supposed to come up with another Elvis sighting and I'm just falling asleep. Cannot connect with another fucking Elvis sighting. But I'm here trying to keep my eyes open and looking at these pictures of Elvis's face superimposed upon the Pope's face. And I'm trying to concoct this story about who *really* calls the shots for the Church in Rome these days. And then the phone rings, and it's Maria Gomez's half brother, and he tells me that Maria is Fidel Castro's son. He's very sincere, the way Pedro can be, and I'm thinking well, all right—okay—it beats the hell out of Elvis in Rome. And it's been a while since we ran a secret son of Castro story, and I'm not sure, but I don't think we ever ran a drag queen secret son of Castro story . . . sure! This one'll play okay. And Pedro goes on to say that Maria plans to seek asylum in the United States and tell the world who she really is and, not incidentally, see if she can start playing better places than the Pink Python. I tell Pedro to come over and see me, and when he gets to my room, he's in bad shape. Shaking and sweating. Says someone sprayed him with something on the street while he was walking over. He feels very weird indeed. He's looking at me very strangely. Like he wants to come on to me, which is not a reaction I see in people too often. I'm four-eight, bald, and weigh ninety pounds. I got a lifelong psoriasis of the face condition and I'm sixty-eight years old at the time. And I'm totally straight to boot. Yet after we swing the deal for the story, Pedro blurts out that despite the fact he is a married man with fourteen children he would sell his soul to the devil just to jump my bones. I just showed him to the door, but a few days later I'm walking down Whitehead Street when a guy runs by me and shoots off some kind of mist in my face as he passes. He seemed to come out of nowhere—a Latino guy—and I'm standing there alone on the street, and I swear to God all I can think of is how much I miss Pedro, whom I only met once in my life. And so here we are today, both of us working on this book about Maria. Serafina and the fourteen kids are in the past—I make sure she gets a check every month. Pedro and I were married in Hawaii in spite of the fact that there is very little information about the spray. How long it lasts, what the aftereffects may be. He's not easy to live with, but the six figures for the book have helped us to bear up with all the uncertainties. As for the actual war on the beach that followed the assassination, I missed the whole show. Pedro and I were honeymooning in Hawaii at the time.

Jackie Hernandez:

All right, I will take your word for the check in the mail even though there are many American jokes about that as well as the coming of the mouth. Just do not think for one second that I do this for nothing. So now I will let you talk to my manager and husband, Alex Delamooche. As you will see for yourself, he is the man who has the goods on everybody.

Alex Delamooche:

I have been a realtor in Key West forty years and friends with President Rollovo just as long. Trashista I know from the time I am a boy in Cuba. Fidel I went to the university with and also shared a house with him when he was in exile. That was in Mexico during the fifties. I have never judged the man. I am a businessman and do not judge politicians. We have remained friends through the years, even though I chose to leave Cuba and Fidel went all ape shit in the sixties. Now I know you will find this incredible, but we used to see each other a lot when Fidel began coming over to Key West in the eighties for his vacations. Key West, Florida, back then. He always came in drag so as not to be recognized. Used to leave his submarine at Stock Island and bicycle over from there. Lots of times when the CIA was sending its crack agents to Havana to kill Fidel, he was actually right here in Key West. You could find him drinking in the bar Rollovo owned, dressed in these hideous old ladies' flower-print dresses. He was very good friends with Rollovo and Trashista was always around too. Fidel loved to dance and tell jokes and do imitations of people like Khrushchev and Kennedy. He used to say he was having the fun he never had in his youth. You see, he was tired of the job by the eighties. He was tired of Cuba. Said Havana had become a toilet bowl. He could get very philosophical. Wonder what life was really all about. And he had a secret wish. A dream that was not so different from other senior citizens. He wanted to retire to Florida! Yes! That's all! Simply spend his retirement in Florida sitting around a pool just like you and me. Well, time goes by and Trashista becomes the big shot he eventually became and Key West secedes from Florida and Trashista tells Fidel it is no longer so impossible for his dream to come true. There is a new U.S. president. Trashista and a lot of other super-rich Cubanos have spent a lot of money to buy this president and put him in the White House. They have also swung the Florida vote, which

the president could not have won the election without. They
convinced the Florida Cubans that this president was mucho
anti-Castro and so they voted for him. But really Trashista and
the boys were only pulling the Cubans' legs. Actually, the personal ambition of the American president was to see if he could
make a real estate killing in Cuba. Which was also the ambition
of Trashista and company. While Fidel just wanted to get the hell
out of Cuba and come to Key West to live, with maybe a few
business dealings in Florida to help pad his retirement fund. Now
not very much happens during the American president's first
term. He has to go on rattling his sword at Fidel because there is
no priority higher than getting the second term. But after that, the
deals begin. All under the table, of course. Secrecy is everything.
The American president and Trashista have their hearts set on
prime waterfront property in Cuba so they will be ready with the
hotels when America begins once again to trade with Cuba. In
return, Fidel is looking at Key West property where he will build
a home, but immediately makes a deal to buy land in northern
Florida under my name. When the time is right, Fidel will have a
lifelong dream realized. He will own a piggy farm in Florida.
And everything from the American president's deals in Cuba to
the piggy farm and whatever Fidel wants in Key West is bank-
rolled by Trashista and friends. Their own reward being almost
half of the Cuban countryside to be converted into tourist havens.
Finally, Fidel makes a decision on his retirement home. He wants
a good large piece of land in Key West that was at one time a
U.S. naval station with a lot of other property attached that was
once U.S. owned. Through the years, the government sold this
land to a private buyer, but now he wants to sell it off. Trashista
tells Fidel there will be no problem in obtaining this land. And
here is where we run into trouble. Because Vincente Rollovo is
his own man who allows no one in on his business dealings. We
are at the point now where the island is clamoring for secession
and Rollovo has been mayor for nearly twenty years. Of course
he has hung in there for so long because of the loyalty of the gay
people on the Island, whom he has courted throughout his career.
In fact, the gays and Rollovo attached their stars to each other as

long ago as the seventies when he represented their business interests on the business guild, which was predominantly redneck at the time. He helped clear the path for the gay business domination of Key West because he wisely figured that with all their money and determination to make the island their own, they were someday bound to succeed. Because he fought the rednecks in the early days, the gays always remembered and supported him, even though he is straight. The gays made him mayor and kept him there. When he heard the first murmurs of the cry for secession, he jumped on them and led the charge. This was bliss to an ambitious politician like Rollovo. Imagine! One leap from mayor of a town to president of a nation! By this time, Key West was overwhelmingly gay because of its well-publicized demand for secession, which would mean a dream gay mecca. By this time, gays were coming into Key West in droves, not for their vacations, but because the word was out that soon the island would be the world's first queer country. And Rollovo encouraged his constituents. He spoke of a gay police force, a gay militia, gay everything. Rollovo was drunk with the thought of it all. His island would not kowtow to the great monster that was the United States. It would take no stand on international issues such as Cuba. It would follow a thoroughly independent isolationist policy. But there's one big hitch. He knows he cannot secede unless the United States allows him to secede, and here is where the new president—a man who finds it impossible to turn down any reimbursement at all for his long years of service to America—here is where Rollovo finds the key to secession. Now you must remember that Trashista has the word of the American president that Fidel is to have the land of his choice in Key West. Rollovo is hardly considered; he is only a small-time mayor. It is believed that since the American president is on a buying spree—under another name of course—in Cuba he can be trusted with Fidel's interests in Key West. And this is true up to a point. But that point becomes negotiable when the big coincidence enters the picture. And the big coincidence is that the American president is looking for his own choice piece of land for a retirement home. And what do you know? No place on the entire planet will do for the president but the old naval station in Key West. The very same land that Trashista has told Fidel will be his just as soon as he can arrange the finances. By this time, Trashista and his friends have spread themselves a little thin with money. Time will be needed to raise the finances for Fidel's land. Meanwhile, the American president, who is completely aware of Fidel's wishes, is talking privately to Rollovo. The American president does not ever part with a dollar of his own; it is one of his principles he will not compromise. Rollovo tells the president he can be of no help to him as long as he is a small-time mayor of a Florida town. But if the town became a nation and Rollovo ruled that nation, it would not be so hard to arrange the naval base for the American president's acquisition. It is the strong wish of the gays on the island that they become independent, and there is no room for doubt as to whom they would choose to lead their new nation. If they ever knew of Rollovo's secret deal with an American president who is supported by the religious American right, the gays' opinion of Rollovo might be different. But they do not know. Just as Trashista and Fidel do not know. Rollovo's thinking is that once he is ruler of Key West Nation he will find a way to deal with gay unappreciation toward a new neighbor whose policies have never favored gays in the United States. If the Key West ruler ever actually allows the president on the island. For the terms are that Key West is allowed to secede first. And then Rollovo produces the president's land. A promise he will honor, but honor with an adjustment of payment. And if the American president can adapt to this adjustment and pay more than Fidel is willing to pay, then he will be welcomed by Rollovo as a new neighbor on the island. How Trashista, who is funding both Fidel and the American president, handles all of this is not a concern of the Key West ruler. And so the controversial referendum (in the U.S. press) is held. Key West votes for secession. The U.S. president accedes to the islanders' wishes and Rollovo comes to power. At the time that the crazy German waitress has kidnapped Trashista, he has just learned of Rollovo's deal with the U.S. president. The president has just learned of the "adjustment" in the deal that he had thought was all set. And Fidel, who has never been known to be in control of his temper over anything American, has just learned he has been double-crossed by the U.S. president. All deals from retirement homes to Cuban sites for American hotels to a piggy farm in North Florida are suddenly on hold. The man with the money is being held at gunpoint in a Key West hotel. Rollovo has had the balls to play one president off another, and the American president is worried about this 400 million dollars of ransom money that would go to Fidel. Would the money go from Fidel to Rollovo for the naval station? The American president is also aware that if the gays of Key West had to choose between Fidel and himself, the gays would probably go for Fidel. He is a rebel, outside the mainstream of international politics. He is of the multicultural minorities. Most gays are not political and have no idea where Fidel stands on gay rights in Cuba. Although there is a small number of Key West gays who are aware of Fidel's past record of inequities and they do not like the man at all. And then there is the matter of the mysterious gay spray that began to appear around the time of the Trashista kidnapping. What was that all about? And finally Maria Gomez—who says she is the son of Castro—is shot to smithereens while she does her impersonation of Marilyn Monroe singing "Happy Birthday" to President Kennedy.

General Lee Maize:

Rumors of this spray Castro was supposed to have had been circulating around the Pentagon for some time. It was designed to be a strategic military paralytic. You could have a plane spray an area with the stuff or ground troops could use it. If, for instance, you blasted a division of troops across a field with the spray, all the enemy had to do was to take it in through their pores or inhale it and they totally lost interest in the invading force. The spray was hypnotic; it made the men turn inward. It caused an overwhelming sexual preoccupation that extended to the man who was closest to you at the time. A soldier would find himself hopelessly sexually stimulated and he would turn for relief to the soldier next to him. One of our men at the Pentagon who was working with biologicals said that there is an element in the spray that induces a kind of a loneliness and longing for an extension of one's self—such as the man next to you. As long as there was a male there, you would become obsessed with this extension of yourself. Or, actually, the extension's extension. A hideous weapon. The men would forget about the goddamn war! The opposing force could easily advance and the only danger posed to them would be uh . . . abominable attraction to their extensions. I rate the destructive potential of this Cuban spray right up there with the most lethal of all biological weapons.

Pedro Gomez:

They began experimenting with it in Cuba in the 1990s. My husband Harry says that *The Nose* finally caught a leak from the Pentagon that identified one of the ingredients as porpoise sperm. You know that porpoises are very, very horny creatures who swing both ways. And *The Nose* also found out that there might have been a highly concentrated essence of four-leaf clover. There was evidence that there were a lot of cargo flights out of Ireland that were landing in Cuba. And American intelligence has supposedly supplied the president with photographic proof that Castro was trying to grow four-leaf clover in the western part of Cuba. *The Nose* says that the president of the United States, at one point, considered bombing the four-leaf clover fields.

Rick Spittle:

The U.S. president was asked at a news conference about Trashista. Would the president allow Trashista to pay 400 million dollars in ransom to save his own life even though that money would legally violate the embargo by going to Cuba? The president answered that the life of a great Cuban American was at stake, and so he was going to allow the transaction. But as I watched him on television I remember thinking that the president had the pained look on his face of a man who knows he has just had his wallet lifted.

Alex Delamooche:

Polls showed that the public was sympathetic toward Trashista, so the president was playing the humanitarian. But Vincente Rollovo had not yet swung the naval station to the president, and the president was very much aware that if 400 million dollars suddenly fell in Fidel's lap, Fidel would be a player again. I think the president was just beginning to realize how deceitful Rollovo really was and that he actually would screw the president of the United States if Fidel suddenly had access to a lot of money.

Jackie Hernandez:

This slut Maria Gomez comes to Key West and *The Nation's Nose* story comes out about how she is the son of Fidel Castro. And you can't even get a ticket to her show at the Pink Python, she is so hot! The son of Fidel Castro in a dress! But a cheap dress, a Kmart dress! Since I am an employee at the club, I am sitting at the bar with my boss, Rick, and we are going to watch this filthy Maria's show. She comes out to do the "Happy Birthday, Mister President" number and all of a sudden, Bang!— Maria's show is seriously disrupted because she has a hole the size of a golf ball in her forehead. She has never looked so good to begin with, but now she is flung back against the curtains with this bloody hole in her head and the wig has been knocked off— a very bad wig!—a cheap wig! And I am thinking that whoever her public relations people are, they certainly know how to grab a headline.

Alex Delamooche:

Fidel knew how many people around the world read *The Nation's Nose*. In fact, he read it too. And he knew a lot of people believed what they read in the magazine. So now he is thinking that there is a perception—irrelevant as to how accurate—that his son has been murdered in a dinky little island ninety miles away from Cuba. And so he is forced to make one of his long rambling speeches full of threats at Key West. He cannot let people believe that he will take the murder of his son lightly. He demands that the government of Key West bring his son's assassin to trial or else face the consequences. He does not say what the consequences are, and Rollovo is not particularly disturbed because he knows Fidel and he knows that Fidel must at least make a speech. Certainly he would not go to war against the island he plans to retire to! But the day after Fidel's speech, Rollovo has something to worry about. Because the U.S. president jumps all over Fidel's speech. And he says that the Trashista ransom deal is off. He simply cannot allow 400 million dollars to go to Cuba at a time when it threatens an ally of the United States. That would be aiding and abetting the enemy. I was sitting at the bar Rollovo still owns in Key West, and I watched the president's statement on television with Rollovo sitting next to me. And right after the president made his statement, Rollovo turned to me and said, "Can you believe it? The president of the United States goes and has a drag queen shot just so he can grab a house in Key West cheap! What's Fidel gonna do about *this*?" Later on that day, I get through to Fidel and he screams into the phone, "That lousy bastard took away my retirement money! How am I gonna pay Rollovo? You can tell Vincente for me that I found out about his secret deals with the president. And you can tell him that even now retaliation is taking place!" He meant the agents he had in Key West who were going around spraying people. Fidel never did trust Rollovo, even though they were drinking buddies, and he had been testing the spray in Key West for weeks before Maria was shot. He was frustrated. There had been the delay while Trashista dealt with financial arrangements, and it had been leaked to him that just maybe there was something funny going on between Rollovo and the American president. He had thought at first—before he learned the truth—that the president could be negotiating secretly with Rollovo to place an American base on the island. And Fidel had set his heart on the site where the Americans would open the base. He got a bit demented, I think. He began planning an attack on Key West to rescue his retirement home. And the first stage was to sneak terrorists onto the island. For which I am eternally grateful because I caught a dose of the spray one night while I was walking past the Pink Python. And after the terrorist ran off, the first man I saw was Jackie walking out of the club. It had been a rare night of drinking for Jackie and she staggered into my sight wearing a diamond-studded jockstrap and a pillbox hat. I had never had a queer moment in my life until that moment. She was hung like a horse, but it was the hat that did it.

Rick Spittle:

I can't say I loved Maria Gomez. When *The Nation's Nose* came out with the Castro's son bit, she drove her price up three times as high as the original agreement before she would play my club. Some thought the gay right had her killed for informing on gays in Cuba, and some thought it was the CIA because the American president wanted an excuse to invade Cuba. You know, a reaction to Castro's crazy war talk, which is what the president expected to hear because so many people thought Maria was Fidel's son. The hit man turned out to be a midget who was a regular patron of the club. We used to call him "Eesnice" because he'd sit in the audience and every time a drag came onstage he would stand on his chair and yell "Ees nice!" He was actually rather sweet, about three feet tall. I think the CIA hired him, myself. And then they tagged him as being hired by the gay right. But he was there at ringside the night Maria came on and she didn't look all that good to Eesnice. She was way overweight and squeezed into one of those see-through dresses. She was supposed to be Marilyn Monroe, but she looked like Bruce Willis in drag. It was pretty ludicrous. She launched into a re-creation of Marilyn singing "Happy Birthday" to President Kennedy back in the sixties. And I'm sitting there thinking about what this turkey is costing me and I watch as little Eesnice scrambles on top of his chair, which is nothing new; he does that all the time. And I'm waiting for him to say the usual "Ees nice" and get down off the chair, but instead he screams, "Ees not so nice!" and then a gun appears from his tiny suit jacket and the next thing I know my star is blown away and

I'm out a lot of money because now nobody is gonna hang around and drink. As for Eesnice, he escaped but never lived to tell his story. Typical cartoon CIA ending. One day—a week later—one of those big beach balls floated in on the tide and they found Eesnice's body inside the ball.

Alex Delamooche:

Fidel believes he has been taken by the American president and Rollovo. He knows the threatening speech he has made was a mistake and it is now possible that the United States would even send troops to Key West to protect the island. If he is to have any chance at all of recapturing his dream retirement home, he must reverse his tactics completely. He cannot take on the United States, so he must neutralize Key West. He must swing the sentiment of the island his way. He must convince the Key Westers that he is on their side and the Americans are the ones they must distrust. He already has his people on the island and he has seen the reports of the spray's effect. So now he must raise the ante with an invasion. But an invasion unlike any in the history of the world. He must send troops to throw the entire population into sexual preoccupation and at the same time propagandize the island with warnings of American homophobia. He must spread the word that to allow American troops onto Key West soil is to guarantee massive gay bashing. Even more serious would be the future residency of the American president. It is the president's secret wish to live on and control the island with his own moral outlook. And this is a politician who was heavily funded by the American religious right. Whereas Fidel's moral outlook will already have been shown by the actions of his invading force, who come to Key West not to maim and kill but to . . . well . . . fuck. If Fidel moves quickly he can get Key West to reject any idea of an American presence. He can foster the idea of himself as an extraordinarily friendly new neighbor. And with the threat of Cuba as a belliger-ent aggressor removed and the revelation of his plans to with-draw his army, leaving only himself to live on the island . . . well, then there is no longer a reason to deprive Trashista of paying off the waitress to spare his own life. Although the waitress was definitely a wild card. And so Fidel raises an army comprised of the 500 most beautiful well-hung men in Cuba. An Army designed to make the population of Key West want to marry each and every soldier. The men will hit the beaches of Key West under air cover that sprays the island. They will not be affected by the spray until they are on Key West because if they were on the spray before the landing time, they would never get to the island to begin with. Although most of the Cuban army is straight, they would take off on a love cruise to the Caribbean with each other if they were sprayed in Cuba. So they will meet the Key West Gay Militia just as the spray is at work on both armies at the same time. And they will bring their message of Cuban love and of American homophobia. And they will bring that message to the beaches of Key West stark naked. With handguns loaded with spray to make sure everyone is sympatico and ready to party with the finest Latinos Cuba has to offer.

General Le Maize:

President Rollovo didn't know what the hell was happening. He was alerted to the fact that these boats full of naked men were nearing the island and so he called up the militia. He sent 500 soldiers, which means that in numbers the two armies were evenly matched. But after just one night of combat, there were no deaths and no wounded among the Cuban army, whereas the Key West Militia listed five men dead of heart attacks and three of strokes. I guess that says something about the constitution of a Key West soldier compared to a Cuban soldier. It might have something to do with the introduction of four-leaf clover into the Cuban diet. I'm not sure. As for the Cuban air cover, they flew in too low to be picked up on radar and they were relatively noiseless since all they did was spray.

Jackie Hernandez:

The next day there were people screwing out in the open all over Key West. I have decided to write a book about that day, and in it I will give the day the detailed attention that is worthy of a scholar. In my book, to be called *Double Fuck,* I will carefully chronicle all that I saw so that future generations will know and learn from our history. I was not going to write this book until I heard that slut Maria's brother had written a book. And then Rick Spittle told me how he had hired the brother to do a drag show at the club. And so then I thought to myself that maybe no one is currently interested in my plans to bring back the style of Jacqueline Onassis. I thought to myself that I owed it to people to tell the *true* story of the war. Do not buy Pedro Gomez's book because in his heart he is still a Catholic with a wife and fourteen children. There will be guilt all over his pages. But I have no guilt. My own allegiance is to historical accuracy, so when you buy my book, you will read all about the sucking and fucking and the double fucks and fist fucks and the coming of the mouth and rivers of sperm that ran in the streets. This book is my gift to the children of Key West—to the future generations—so that they will know the struggle we have endured on our island. And so that they will know just how hard their fathers fought so that our nation could remain free.

Alex Delamooche:

The next day after the war on the beach there was a three-way telephone conference in the office of the president of Key West. Vincente Rollovo, the American president, and Fidel Castro took part in this conference. I was there representing Fidel's real estate interests and also to translate his more obscure outbursts of Spanish, which were due to the fact that he had been drinking. Not one of the three leaders knew what to do. It was apparent that Rollovo had lost control over the island and of himself also. The entire time he was on the phone with the two presidents he had his houseboy on his lap and was playing with the boy's diddly do. The American president and Fidel, after an hour of arguing, finally decided to put all real estate deals on hold until the Trashista matter was resolved. Fidel felt weakened because of the desertion of his troops who, in the person of the commander, had informed him on the phone that they had no intention of ever returning to Cuba. They were all very happy where they were on Key West. It was quite apparent to the American president that he no longer had any excuse to place troops in Key West. The islanders had turned completely anti-American overnight because of the successful propaganda put out by the Cuban soldiers. The Cuban army had come to believe this propaganda and were now fearful that they would be gay bashed by the Americans too. Fidel and the American president agreed that the biggest issue they had to confront was that of exposure. Vera Verboten, the crazy German waitress who held Trashista at gunpoint, was going to issue a statement that day. The world media were waiting to hear what she would say. The American president entertained thoughts of impeachment and Fidel believed the Cuban people would rise up against him if it turned out that Trashista had spilled the beans to the waitress.

Jackie Hernandez:

All right now! Get your checkbook ready! Vera never made the statement she said she would make. Instead she blew Trashista's brains out and then turned the gun on herself, which I would have advised her not to do if I had had the chance. An overdose of pills taken in an air-conditioned room is so much better because you will be found looking well groomed and cool as a cucumber. But always remember to go to the bathroom before taking the overdose or else you will be found looking more like chopped squash than a cucumber. But anyway, word was sent to me that she wanted me to bring up wine before she would make her statement. So I get off the elevator with the wine and the bill in a good mood because Vera has turned into such an excellent tipper. And just as I am about to knock, I hear her scream, "WHAT? A PIGGY FARM IN FLORIDA?" And now we come to my secret and the reason why I tell you to keep the checkbook ready. Also the reason why my book deal was so fabulous. In the suite, along with the disgraceful-looking bodies, I found a tape. Vera had been recording Trashista. There have been many attempts to take this tape away from me, but none have succeeded. Until I just now decided to tell you of the existence of this tape, only Alex Delamooche and my publisher knew I had this little piece of gold. The three presidents can go on denying that the Key West war never happened all they want. They can deny all the rest too. But I have the tape. Everything you would like to know. For instance, Trashista knew all about Fidel's gay spray. And he knew of the plans that Fidel had, and still has to this day, for the United States. But before I continue, I will lend you my pen for the checkbook that you have finally taken from your pocket.

Survival on the Glacial Slide

The composition of a large canvas that cost more than he can afford—that he should not have thought of starting so close to summer. Most of the picture still inside his head.

High up on the left, a large off-white house set back on young green grass of lawn that covers a third of the width and length of the canvas.

The new even green of midspring, the unflaked white of new paint. And then grays and dirty whites—unkempt and scruffy yard-sale coat of the adult coyote on the perfect lawn. Two babies licked clean tumbling in play at her feet. She is looking toward a forest of popping green buds that will cover the last third length and width of the canvas.

Beneath the lawn that was carved from the forest is a road that travels across the canvas. A concrete stream of creamy tan road to divide the length of the canvas in half.

And a beach below the road, centered by a gray cottage, chipped and faded by salty winds, the birthplace of the plans upon this page. On the small space of porch a man with a beard, coyote gray, dressed in red flannel shirt and blue jeans.

Off-whites of house and drab coyote—greens of lawn and forest buds—cream of road and beach—aged grays of cottage, man, and beast (with grays that shine on playful babies)—blue jeans and the bay—the worn red of shirt to harmonize with a wandering fox, reddish orange (like the sun already gone), in the corner below.

The man sits in a rocker—its twin empty beside him and nudged by the wind that rocks in place of the companion whose chair it used to be.

The bottom of the canvas—the remaining fifth of space is reserved for the indented shore of the bay curving concave in the center—two small seabirds (just remembered), chrome against a twilight gray and so nearly matching caps for the swirling tide below. And there will be a drama played by the fox standing where the beach begins to rise in the corner, in the east.

This is the composition that plays in the mind of rueful countenance who whispers to the wind in the chair beside his own. The painting, only just started, is upon the easel inside the cottage and cannot be completed until fall. When the coyote takes back the residence across the road above and the fox is free again to roam the beach, leaving single-file prints, then they will hear the cough and sputter of a painter's car crammed with canvases, easels, and paints.

And now a warm southwest wind blows across this peninsula of glacial remains, ruffling the fur of the coyote who leads her babies to the forest. Ruffles, too, the long hair of the painter soon to be respectably barbered for the tourist season. And ripples the bristled coat of the fox now deserting the beach that will bed the onslaught of glistening burning human bodies.

The painter speaks to the rocking wind of the similarity at a certain time of twilight between the color of air and coyote coats. Thinks how he can blend the two. And meditates upon the colors of silence—colors to convey serenity that is temporary like morning fog that can look so deep and permanent and then is gone in a blink. He wants to communicate a transient peace hovering in the road to signify that the animals are safe only until the green leaves return. Wishes he could somehow hint at lethal threats that rush the road like crazed metallic predators in summer. The season's traffic that steals away the lives of disoriented animals. The business of summer that takes away the suddenly high-valued home of the painter.

He muses about the forest to the east of the vacant house above, how he must suggest the future in thickening greens that will hide the coyote by the time of the house owner's return. An interesting subject for a painter—intimations of the future through colors. To suggest a forthcoming density of green that will shield the animals through summer. On canvas, buds of the trees, some unopened, should be set close together so that one can imagine a June roof of green. And is it possible to create the swiftness of time through paints? The strokes of speed with which the summer will come and go? The imminent yet leap-frogging return of autumn though it is still spring? Maybe there can be an indication of lightheartedness in the mother coyote, a knowing look of exile as temporary. A reclamation of the entire estate is not so very far away. She could be portrayed in a pose of assurance, poised in high step while the babies tumble. Yes, and have one baby nipping another gleefully while the mother steps like a queen toward the castle of green, repainted yet again for another summer.

Ah, but the stark contrast of a fox in the lower corner, so nervous trotting the beach with single-file steps, small and low to the sand, looking like a rare pedigree of domestic dog. Tense, delicate pointy face, moving east but caught with a nose full of scents born on the west wind that has him looking back over his shoulder. A haunted sense to this red fox, of lingering despair, loneliness for a vixen crushed by Labor Day traffic in the late summer of last year. Coat bristled by the wind that sways the empty creaking rocker beside the painter who watches from above.

There is space on the lower right side of the canvas for an inlet. With a stroke of the brush the painter will alter erosion—put back what was lost on the concave shore. The beach will have an even line of sand with an inlet on the right where the fox has paused. There will be a sandbar and the swirl of tides—small pieces of beach tearing away, dissolving into grains of sand that flow to stock the eastern tip. Crystals of paw prints to sail the bay in the light of a horn moon—the slides collection to lie like fine china upon the continental shelf.

The fact that the fox looks away from the painter in order to absorb the news on the wind reveals familiarity. For an entire winter the fox has passed the den above, has come to know the aromas of food, the smell of burning wood contained, not threat-ening. And the man rocking at twilight is now a part of the beach, a colorful figure who sits up there upon the table of sand and does nothing but stare into the cold blue sea.

And the painter above stirs restlessly, brooding upon the time of waste ahead living in town above a garage. A stone's throw away from a house of eyes watching suspiciously a graying man without a house to call his own. Eyes that scout his routine for the means to pay them rent.

With a mind like a fox whose every move is self-erasure, he always moves the unsold canvases into the summer dump under cover of darkness. Never mentions the paintings to the landlord who would double the security payment if he knew. Speaks only of business at the local restaurant to allay rental fears. The job in a kitchen is the only identity he promotes so that he can live above the garage until September when the incredibly high rent of the cottage plummets. At least this year there is only the canvases to hide. At least this year there is no other artist caught in the steel clamps of an unspringable trap. And passed off as allergic to spooked and fearful eyes.

The summer was an annual herring run toward autumn, an upstream swim against financial currents that washed over the bridge with the arrival of the tourists. He was always drained of time to paint so that he could meet the price of escalated rents. His collection of work included the quilt blanket colors of fall, the stark gnarled lines inside the pierce of winter light, the infantile greens of spring thaw. But no canvas heated the eyes with a summer day's profusion of overgrowth and decay. And by August he always had stomach problems, all his unreleased visions having aborted and run to acid. His paralyzed brain would reflect the blank of canvas that swelled to dominate his room like the stricken blind eyes of the god inside himself.

And now he sits in the lengthening lavenders of evening, watching the dark rain down, released in dots from above by a pointillist connecting the night. The wind has shifted to blow from the north, and he shudders free from the sense of existing on canvas. Watches the fox whose head revolves like a weather vane to gather northern scents. Long and low and fine-boned, on his way east to where the beach they both inhabit at this moment will some day flow. And the gallery of the painter's mind, as variable as the wind, shows the coyote north on the lawn across the road. An animal so obvious and yet still unknown to so many who live out here. One day the coyote inside his soul howled upon hearing the owner of the off-white house say that he had never even seen a coyote.

His thoughts blow around again to the fox pinned to the canvas of sand. A drama brought down on the north wind and broadcasted in the quivering nose. Requiring a change in course. He trots northeast and the painter knows the reason why. To lose the danger on the north wind, the fox will travel up beyond dunes to a large concrete parking lot. Entering from the west, the indication to a predator would be that the fox is on his way east. But the concrete of the lot leaves no prints and very little scent. Nor does the creamy tan concrete road that adjoins the lot offer up much in the way of directional clues. And on that road, so lethal in memory, he will double back west to lose an enemy.

A nod of farewell and approval to the fox and up from his chair with a quick pat on the arm of the chair beside him, rocking impatiently now in the wind. Up to pack and preserve those prints so carefully crafted to reveal his whereabouts, to show the way of his life.

But pauses at the cottage door. A sense that it trespasses the laws of survival to stop and preserve. And finds himself titillated by an effeminate rush that speaks of complicity in a piteous relationship. The wonder of an animal who tries so hard to attract the scavengers of his beauty.

ABOUT THE AUTHOR

William Rooney lives in various parts of the United States, preferring not to linger long in any one location. He has been writing novels, unrecognized and unpublished, for twenty-five years. He was, early in his life, in the U.S. Air Force for a brief spell before resigning, claiming chronic boredom as the reason for his premature departure. But for acting on the impulse of his logic, he was penalized by having to serve a month in jail before he was finally discharged. He then went to New York City and became an actor, landing a part in Brian Friel's *The Mundy Scheme* on Broadway in 1969. He quit acting after the play closed because he realized that American culture would require him (with his boyish looks) to play moronic juveniles in pathetic comedies until the day would come (maybe twenty years later) when it would take a pound of pancake just to cover the lines in his face. In all the years that followed he has traveled quite a bit, supporting himself by bartending (even spending one night working behind a bar in Paris, speaking absolutely not a word of French). His life's ambition is to own a chunk of land which he would populate with dogs, none of which would be up for sale.

Order Your Own Copy of
This Important Book for Your Personal Library!

ROONEY'S SHORTS

_____in hardbound at $39.95 (ISBN: 1-56023-954-9)

_____in softbound at $14.95 (ISBN: 1-56023-150-5)

COST OF BOOKS_____

OUTSIDE USA/CANADA/
MEXICO: ADD 20%_____

POSTAGE & HANDLING_____
(US: $3.00 for first book & $1.25
for each additional book)
Outside US: $4.75 for first book
& $1.75 for each additional book)

SUBTOTAL_____

IN CANADA: ADD 7% GST_____

STATE TAX_____
(NY, OH & MN residents, please
add appropriate local sales tax)

FINAL TOTAL_____
(If paying in Canadian funds,
convert using the current
exchange rate. UNESCO
coupons welcome.)

☐ **BILL ME LATER:** (\$5 service charge will be added)
(Bill-me option is good on US/Canada/Mexico orders only;
not good to jobbers, wholesalers, or subscription agencies.)

☐ Check here if billing address is different from
shipping address and attach purchase order and
billing address information.

Signature_____

☐ **PAYMENT ENCLOSED:** $_____

☐ **PLEASE CHARGE TO MY CREDIT CARD.**

☐ Visa   ☐ MasterCard   ☐ AmEx   ☐ Discover
☐ Diner's Club

Account #_____

Exp. Date_____

Signature_____

Prices in US dollars and subject to change without notice.

NAME _____

INSTITUTION _____

ADDRESS _____

CITY _____

STATE/ZIP _____

COUNTRY _____ COUNTY (NY residents only) _____

TEL _____ FAX _____

E-MAIL_____
May we use your e-mail address for confirmations and other types of information? ☐ Yes   ☐ No

Order From Your Local Bookstore or Directly From
The Haworth Press, Inc.
10 Alice Street, Binghamton, New York 13904-1580 • USA
TELEPHONE: 1-800-HAWORTH (1-800-429-6784) / Outside US/Canada: (607) 722-5857
FAX: 1-800-895-0582 / Outside US/Canada: (607) 772-6362
E-mail: getinfo@haworthpressinc.com
PLEASE PHOTOCOPY THIS FORM FOR YOUR PERSONAL USE.

BOF96